OTHER YEARLING BOOKS YOU WILL ENJOY:

FOURTH-GRADE CELEBRITY, *Patricia Reilly Giff*
THE GIRL WHO KNEW IT ALL, *Patricia Reilly Giff*
LEFT-HANDED SHORTSTOP, *Patricia Reilly Giff*
LOVE, FROM THE FIFTH-GRADE CELEBRITY,
Patricia Reilly Giff
RAT TEETH, *Patricia Reilly Giff*
THE WINTER WORM BUSINESS, *Patricia Reilly Giff*
TOOTSIE TANNER, WHY DON'T YOU TALK?,
Patricia Reilly Giff
BETSY'S BUSY SUMMER, *Carolyn Haywood*
BETSY'S PLAY SCHOOL, *Carolyn Haywood*
BETSY AND MR. KILPATRICK, *Carolyn Haywood*

YEARLING BOOKS/YOUNG YEARLINGS/YEARLING CLASSICS are designed especially to entertain and enlighten young people. Patricia Reilly Giff, consultant to this series, received the bachelor's degree from Marymount College. She holds the master's degree in history from St. John's University, and a Professional Diploma in Reading from Hofstra University. She was a teacher and reading consultant for many years, and is the author of numerous books for young readers.

For a complete listing of all Yearling titles,
write to Dell Readers Service,
P.O. Box 1045, South Holland, IL 60473.

D0109164

Five-Finger Discount

Barthe DeClements

A Yearling Book

Published by
Dell Publishing
a division of
Bantam Doubleday Dell Publishing Group, Inc.
666 Fifth Avenue
New York, New York 10103

The trademark Yearling® is registered in the U.S. Patent and Trademark Office.

The trademark Dell® is registered in the U.S. Patent and Trademark Office.

ISBN: 0-440-40321-9

Printed in the United States of America

August 1990

10 9 8 7 6 5 4 3 2 1

CWO

This book is dedicated to my daughter, Nicole,
and our friend, Nancy Wilson.

My thanks to Kris Kellogg and her students
at Benjamin Rush Elementary who coached me
on party games, swirlies, clothes, Swatches,
and ten-speeds and made me an illustrated
dictionary of their slang.

My grateful thanks also to my son,
Christopher Greimes, and my daughter,
Nicole Southard, who critiqued the manuscript.

1   The Tree House and the Trashed Car   1

2   Lookin' Good   11

3   King Me   19

4   The Blackmailer   25

5   The Prisoner's Kid   31

6   Smoke the Little Toad   39

7   Party Down   45

8   The Swirly   51

9   Mrs. Nettle's Office   61

10   View from the Tree House   71

11   Five-Finger Discount   77

12   A Mean Face   85

13   Lost and Found   93

14   Something in Me   101

15   Dad's Home   109

16   Close Call   115

17   Wishing on the North Star   123

1

The Tree House
and the Trashed Car

After Mom left for work, I finished emptying the packing boxes. The house we'd just moved into was okay. Not great, but okay. A little shacky, but the rent fitted Mom's waitress salary and the bit Dad sent.

I wandered around the living room, dragging my heels on the worn rug. Nothing more to do inside. It was time to check out the neighborhood.

I walked south past two blocks of big greenhouses that some nursery owned, I guess. Then there was a Coast to Coast store that took up a half a block, then Highway 2, and after that a bunch of old houses. Not a kid my age anywhere. I even stopped and looked in back of the old houses to see if there were any basketball hoops. Not one.

I took a right turn at a gas station and whoa! The sweetest find possible. A construction site! Lumber, boxes of nails, bags of cement, rolls of tar paper. And it was Saturday. The fir tree in my new yard was going to have a tree house in it before this weekend was over.

I didn't get it built without a lot of sweat, though. First, I stuffed my pockets with nails and picked up small sticks to make a ladder on the tree trunk. There was a hammer in our garage, but no saw. So when I went back to the site, I had to paw through a pile of boards to find ones the right size. I lugged those home, six at a time, and made one last trip for a half roll of roofing paper.

I thought the worst part was over when I had the loot piled in my yard. But it was no joke hauling up planks between prickly branches. And the branches were so green and bouncy, it was hard to pound nails in them.

I'd just managed to get about a fourth of the platform built, when a teenager came out of the house next door. He had some bolts and a screwdriver in his hand. I figured he was going to work on his car. The car was in his driveway, which was right beside my tree. It was a cool car, black and slinky.

I didn't want him to hear me hammering, so I slipped out of the tree, went in my back door, and got a doggy bag out of the refrigerator. Chicken slices wrapped in plastic were inside the bag. Good. I hate it when Mom brings me home ham. All that slimy, white fat stuck in the pink meat.

By the time I'd made a chicken sandwich and eaten it, I thought the guy next door might be gone. He wasn't. Through the living room window I could see him with a girl. She looked like she was giving him a bad time. Interesting.

I closed the back door softly, crept across the yard, and went up the tree by the side of my house. The teenagers were too involved in their argument to no-

2

tice me. I stretched belly down on the planks where I could see the whole show.

The girl was circling around the guy yelling her head off. "Just tell me, then. Just tell me why I always see you with her. Tell me that, if you're just good friends."

The guy casually backed against his car. "We're taking auto shop together and we get talking about engines." He waved his screwdriver around as he explained. "We're interested in the same things. It's simple. Can't you understand?"

"I should be able to. As long as it's simple," the girl said through clenched teeth.

The guy shrugged, then bent down to finish screwing an air dam on the front of his car. The girl stood behind him, steaming. "And I suppose you can't help it if she has gorgeous red hair?"

The guy didn't bother to turn around. He just shrugged again. That did it. The girl leaned over and bit him. She bit him right on the shoulder. Even up in the tree where I was, I could see his T-shirt dent in under her teeth.

That got his attention all right. He whirled around, and I thought she was going to get it in the face with the screwdriver. Instead, he jabbed it twice in the air. "What the . . . ? What do you think you're doing, you stupid witch?" He took a big breath, lowered his arm, rubbed his shoulder, and said slow and low, "That does it. That's the last time you're doing that."

"Fine with me," she said. "But first I'll give your precious car a little good-bye." And before he could do anything about it, she climbed up on the hood and did a tiptoe twirl. She had on boots, too. And everywhere she twirled the black paint cracked under her feet.

He grabbed for her. She was too quick, though. She hopped off the other side of the hood and zipped down the street. He took a short spurt after her, but must have figured she had too big of a lead. He turned back to his car, brushed the chipped paint off the hood, and stood sadly staring at the streaks of gray undercoating.

I figured the show was over and was about to ease off the platform, when a girl about my age came out the front door of the house. She had long black hair. A big red ribbon was stuck in the back of it, which made her look sort of nerdy. She walked across the lawn to the driveway where the guy was mourning over his trashed car. "Matt," she said to him, "Mom says you're to drive me over to Aunt Jean's."

"She does, huh? Well, my car isn't fixed."

"When's it going to be fixed?"

"Who knows."

The girl tilted her head to the side. "Well, are you going to take me or not?"

The guy was still staring at the scratches and not really paying attention to the girl.

"Well?" She said it a little louder this time.

He glanced up. "Why don't you just stick around here?"

"Bor—ring!"

She went back in the house, and a few seconds later a woman came out. I figured she was their mother, because she had the same blue eyes and black hair the

4

kids did, except her hair was shorter than the girl's. When she got over to the car, she looked down at the hood. "What in the world happened?"

"Barb," the guy said.

"Barbara?"

"Ya, she did a farewell dance."

"Up on the car?" She gaped at the guy like she was having trouble believing it. "Well, I hope it was a real farewell. That girl is completely unstable."

"Tell me about it," he said.

The mother shook her head three or four times. "The trouble with this car is that it just crumbles like cardboard."

"It's fiberglass, Mom."

"I don't know why your father let you buy it."

"Because it'd been whacked and was cheap. Only it isn't going to be cheap to repaint it. That's the end of getting my band uniform cleaned."

"What do you mean?" his mom asked him sharply. "That uniform's a mess. You can't march in it like that. Can't you just touch those scratches up in shop?"

"No, you can't just touch the scratches up. The whole thing has to be sanded down and spray-painted. And the shop teacher isn't going to give me the paint."

"How much does the paint cost?"

The guy shrugged. "I don't know. But it'll cost more than the ten dollars I've got for the cleaners."

While the mother thought a minute, I began to smile to myself. This guy was reeling her in like a fish. Before she knew it, she was going to be paying for a paint job that would cover the hood and the air dam too.

5

"How did you get orange pop all over your uniform anyway?" she asked.

"Barb," he said.

"Oh, for heaven's sake. This better be the last of that girl."

"It is," he agreed. He was talking to his mom real nice at this point.

"Well, I'll get the uniform cleaned. You take Grace on over to her cousins. She needs to be with some other kids her age."

Before his mom could turn to go back in the house, the guy said quickly, "What about the spray paint? I can't leave the car outside with these scratches on it."

"Oh, well. Bring me the bill from your auto shop and I'll pay whatever it is over ten dollars." She started to leave him.

"I'm about outa gas and it's fifteen miles to Aunt Jean's."

His mom frowned. This was obviouly getting to be much, but she didn't know how to get unhooked. "I'll give Grace the money for gas."

After she went in the house, the guy didn't look so unhappy. He finished bolting the air dam to his car just as Grace came back out. She surveyed the finished job. "Cool. That thing sticking out in front makes your car look like a racer. Where'd you get it?"

"The wrecking yard," he told her. "Where's the money for gas?"

She handed it over to him before they got in the car and drove away. I scooted back against the trunk of the tree and sat there thinking about the neighbors. I figured Grace must be ten or eleven like me and her

6

brother was about sixteen. The way he operated reminded me of my dad.

Funny, I'd heard my grandma tell Mom that Dad would stay sixteen for the rest of his life. But it's no use worrying about what Grandma says. She hates my dad.

I got down out of the tree and started poking boards up through the prickly branches again. I had the platform circled halfway around the tree trunk when it got too dark to work any more.

It was late Sunday afternoon before I had the platform finished. I was beat and ready to quit. But when I stood on the ground and looked up, I could see parts of the unpainted planks through the branches. The only thing to do was to haul up the roofing paper.

On Monday I'd have to register at the new school. By the time I got home the kids next door might be outside. And if I left the raw planks up there all week, they might spot them.

It was dark again when I finished nailing the tar paper to the bottom of the planks and around the sides and up over the branches above the platform. It made a neat nest, though. And dry. I sat up there enjoying my secret perch until my growling stomach drove me down.

Before my mom got home from the restaurant, I was in bed. No need for her to know how late I watch TV. No need for her to get a chance to remind me to wake her up early to take me to school.

It was about eleven in the morning when she rushed into the kitchen. "Jerry Junior! Why didn't you get me up? Now you'll only have a half day of school."

"Forget that," I said. "Let's just get me registered

and then go to the Brethren House and check out their clothes."

She chewed on her nails a minute. "I guess that's a good idea. If we register first you can see what the other kids are wearing."

I figured she'd think it was a good idea. She always likes me to look like the other kids, even if it has to be in clothes donated by the church ladies to the Brethren House.

Silver King Elementary looked like all the other schools in the small towns around Seattle. One-story buildings splattered out in a maze. Mom parked in front and we wandered around the paths until we saw a little sign that said Office. A man with glasses and a big nose was at the counter inside. "May I help you?" he asked.

Mom handed him the withdrawal papers from my last school, which were sealed in a large manila envelope. I was afraid to look at the man while he read the papers. I didn't know what was written in there under Father's Occupation and Father's Address.

It was safer just to stare out the window at the kids going to lunch recess. They were dressed about the same as in my old school. Mostly sweatshirts, T-shirts, jeans, and running pants.

A woman came out of an inner office marked Principal.

"Hello," she said. "I'm Wilma Nettle."

Before my mom could say anything, the man said, "This is Mrs. Johnson and our new fifth-grade

8

student, Gerald Johnson, Jr. Or would you rather be called Jerry?"

"Jerry," I told him after I'd nodded politely at Mrs. Nettle. Which one was the principal? I wondered.

I asked my mom that when we were back out in the car.

"Mrs. Nettle, of course," she said.

"Seems weird to have a woman principal and a man secretary," I said.

"I don't see anything weird about it," she snapped.

I knew better than to get into that with her. I stared out of the car window as she drove out of Snohomish and down Highway 2 toward the town of Monroe. As we came to the edge of Monroe, I saw the sign that pointed up the hill. The sign that said REFORMATORY.

I focused my eyes on the dashboard while Mom drove to the Brethren House. I didn't want to catch sight of the top of the hill and the watchtower on the corner of the wall. It made my insides squeeze into a lead lump just knowing my dad was inside that prison.

9

2

Lookin' Good

I flipped through the jackets that were hanging on the side wall of the Brethren House. Two other boys, who looked like they were in junior high, were pawing through the rack of clothes too. When I pulled out a gray denim, one of the guys poked his friend. "Hey, there's a Generra jacket!"

The friend hung his neck forward to get a good look at the jacket in my hands. "You're right," he said and reached out to take it.

I slipped a couple feet to the side and put the jacket on. It was neat. It had a zipper pocket on one of the sleeves and a double front. There were drawstrings on the outside collar that you could pull to keep the wind out. The cuffs hung down over my hands, but I could turn those up.

"That's too big for you," the guy who'd made a grab for the jacket said. "It's my size."

"Back off!" I told him.

Mom joined us in a hurry. "You don't need to snarl," she said to me.

So much for what she knows. I learned a long time

11

ago from Rattler, one of my dad's friends, that if you're fierce enough, bigger guys leave you alone. Rattler's short and skinny, but he's real mean. At least he seems real mean. I asked Dad once if Rattler ever hurt anyone.

My dad laughed. "Naw, he just keeps everyone off guard by acting like he would. I only saw him in one fight. The other guy was cleaning him, but Rattler wouldn't give up. Finally the guy just dropped Rattler and walked away. He felt stupid beating on him."

Actually, there were two things I learned from Rattler. One, snarl if anyone bigger comes at you, and two, don't back away from a fight. You get over cuts and bruises, but if it gets out you're chicken, you'll get pounded on all the time.

The kid who wanted the jacket stood there scowling at me. All the stuff at the House was free for prisoners' families. You were in luck if you found something really good.

I turned my back on the kid and walked over to a table that had some sweatshirts on it. Most of them were too small or were pukey colors. There was one plain yellow one that was okay. "You got any money?" I asked Mom.

"A little bit. Why?"

"So we can go to the hobby shop and get a bottle of paint I can use on cloth."

"What are you going to write?" She hated my Party Animal T-shirt.

"You don't have to worry," I told her. "I'm just going to print my name on it. I saw a kid at Silver King with his name on the back of a Coca-Cola sweat."

12

There was a hobby shop right in the middle of Monroe. Mom bought me the fabric paint. And knowing my handwriting isn't great, she bought me some stencils too. Neat ones of the alphabet that were more like written letters than printed ones.

I stretched the sweatshirt out on Mom's ironing board. She slipped wax paper underneath the back of the shirt so the paint wouldn't bleed through to the ironing board cover. I worked very carefully. The bottle of paint was about as big as an aspirin bottle and I wanted to be sure I could stencil in my whole name.

When the paint was dry, I put on the sweatshirt and went to look at myself in the mirror on the bathroom door. I had to twist around to see the back of the shirt. There was my name in big navy blue letters. I especially liked the E that was made with two curls. Cool, man.

Even though it was October, it was too warm out the next morning to wear a jacket and a sweatshirt, so I left the jacket home. Mrs. Nettle had given me a little map of the Snohomish School District. There was a red circle around my bus stop.

The bus stop was in the opposite direction from the construction site. I had just passed the white house next door and the white church on the other side of that, when I heard a girl call, "Hey, Jerry!"

At first I was startled to hear my name and then I remembered it was on my shirt. I turned around to see the girl next door hurrying toward me. When she caught up, she said, "You just moved in, didn't you?"

13

I nodded.

"What teacher you got?"

"Hillard," I said.

"No kiddin'? That's who I have, too."

"What's Hillard like?" I asked.

"Well." Grace tilted her head to the side, the way I'd seen her do when she was talking to her brother. "He's kinda hard to describe. He isn't crabby and he'll help you if you ask him to. But most of the time he's sort of out of it. He sits at his desk and reads books."

"What do you guys do while he's reading?"

"We do our work," she said.

Weird, I thought.

There was a bench with a roof over it at the bus stop. Grace plunked her books down, took a mirror and comb out of her purse, and undid the ribbon clip in her hair. She held the mirror out to me. "Hold this," she said.

I backed away, taking a quick look up and down the street.

"Here! Take it." She sounded disgusted. "Nobody else comes to this stop and the bus isn't due for three minutes. You're safe."

I took the mirror. Grace bent over so she could peer into it while she combed one side of her long, black hair. She pulled that half of her hair around to the back of her head and pinned it there with the clip. Presto, the nerdy look was gone.

She stood up and took the mirror from my hand. "Isn't it better?" she asked.

I shrugged. "It's okay, I guess. Why do you wear it that dumb way around your house?"

"Because of my mom. She's hung up on how my brother and I look to people." As she stuffed her ribbon, mirror, and comb in her purse, she watched my face to see if I understood. I guess she thought she should explain herself more. "Because I'm a PK, you know."

I didn't know.

The bus pulled up at our stop. Grace got on first and joined a bunch of girls sitting on the backseat. I sat down next to some little kid with big glasses. He looked out the window all the way to school. That was all right with me because I was trying to figure out what PK meant.

Prisoner's kid? I keep my mouth shut about my dad being in prison. I could understand how Grace's mom was hung up on how she looked to people, but wouldn't she want Grace to keep her mouth shut too?

The work was about the same at Silver King as it had been at my old school in Renton. Mr. Hillard started off math by putting a problem on the board. Eight times nine thousand, three hundred, sixty four.

"How do I start this problem?" he asked us.

Pete, the kid next to me, raised his hand. "You multiply eight times four."

"Then what do I do?" Mr. Hillard wanted to know.

Grace, who sat clear across the room from me, raised her hand. "Put a two down and carry the three."

"And where do I put that?"

"Put it above the four," Grace said.

Mr. Hillard did.

15

When his multiplication example was finished, and Mr. Hillard was certain everybody understood the process, he assigned us a page of problems in the math book. I took out a piece of paper from my notebook, but I didn't know how to head it. Pete pointed to a poster up on the wall.

> **HEADING**
> Joe Schmoe   (on the left side of the
>   top line)
> Sept. 2, 1988
> Science p. 20 #1–10
> (skip one space)
> I.

I very carefully made my heading exactly the same, except for changing the date to October and subject to math. I didn't want trouble in this school. I didn't want to have to be corrected about anything.

While we worked on our math problems, Mr. Hillard sat at his desk reading. Just like Grace had said. The room was quiet until about two minutes before recess. And then the kids started to rustle.

Mr. Hillard put his book away, told us our papers would be due the first thing the next morning, and called on a girl named Kathy to dismiss the class. First, Kathy handed out library passes. Next, she handed out balls. Pete took a basketball.

When everybody had what they wanted, Kathy looked all around the room to find a table where the kids were sitting up straight. Pete's and my table was the third one to get dismissed. On the way out to the playground, Pete asked me if I liked to play basketball. "Sure," I said. One of the best things about our new house was that it had a hoop on the garage.

We started out playing one-on-one. After a while two other kids joined us. One kid was a loudmouth who kept trying to make impossible shots. I caught the ball under the hoop when he missed, twisted my body around, and went for a lay-up.

"Way to go!" Pete hollered. "You made it."

"Hey, Jerry, what's your secret power?" the loudmouth called out.

I just raised my eyebrows and dribbled the ball. No use letting them know how much time I had to practice by myself.

I was feeling pretty good after recess. But as the day dragged on through social studies, reading, and health, the droopy, stuffy classroom feeling came over me. I kept glancing at the clock as it crawled toward three twenty. While Kathy dismissed us, Mr. Hillard smiled for the first time that day.

On the bus I thought some more about what PK meant. I couldn't think of anything else but prisoner's kid. At least nothing else that you'd have to explain about.

Grace got off the bus after me. "Hey, wait up," she told me.

I waited while she put her books on the bench, loosened the clip, let her hair fall down around her face, and pinned the ribbon back on top of her head.

"You mind looking like Little Bo-Peep?" I asked.

She shrugged. "There's no other kids in the neighborhood and it keeps my mom off my back."

17

"Do you just come out and tell everyone you're a PK?"

"Not everyone. But people find out about my dad anyway."

It sounded like PK meant prisoner's kid, all right. We walked along silently until we reached Grace's house. Then I said, "I guess I'm a PK too."

She looked startled. "You are? You don't seem like one."

I hoped not.

3

King Me

I looked in the mailbox when I got home. I didn't really think there'd be any letters so soon, but there were two. One was addressed to Occupant advertising a hardware sale and one was addressed to me from my dad.

Before I went up to the tree house to read the letter, I dumped my books in the bedroom and grabbed my jacket. Clouds had spread across the sky and it was getting cold outside. On the way to the back door I stopped by the refrigerator and got an apple. There was a pile of them, because Mom had brought a whole sackful back from the Brethren House.

Up on my platform I settled against the trunk of the fir tree and ripped open the envelope. Dad wrote that he had a new prison job with Redwood Industries. They made Union Bay clothing. Dad said anytime I saw a Union Bay label on something, I'd know it came from the Monroe Reformatory and maybe he'd made part of it. I wondered what part. Did he work on a sewing machine?

He figured with the new job he'd be able to send

19

more money home. Maybe even two hundred dollars a month. Mom would be glad of that, I thought.

At the end of the letter Dad wrote that he loved me and for me to be sure to watch the North Star when the sky was clear, because he would be watching it too.

He never let Mom bring me along on her visits. Not that he's a murderer or anything. He just didn't want me to see my old man in jail. Instead, we'd watch the North Star together, he said. And he reminded me in every letter.

Well, it was too cloudy to see the North Star this night. I stuffed the letter in my pocket, finished my apple, and threw the core into the neighbors' driveway. I was about to climb out of the tree when I spotted a man coming across the neighbors' backyard from the white church.

I heard his steps going up to their porch and then a door open. Did he just walk in? Maybe he was the preacher in the church. Maybe he came often to counsel the family. Mom had gotten counseling at the Brethren House when Dad first went to prison.

I craned my neck to see into the neighbors' kitchen window, but the blinds were slanted down. It was getting too cold to sit in the tree much longer. I went in the house, turned on the TV, and watched Donahue run around with his microphone.

The next morning, school started out the same as the day before. But Mr. Hillard had a little surprise for us in math. He had bought three pumpkins. A big one, a middle-size one, and a tiny one. We were to guess how much each pumpkin weighed.

There was a scale on the shelf where the pumpkins

sat. Mr. Hillard told us we could help ourselves guess by weighing other comparable things on the scale. But weighing the pumpkins was out.

I tilted back in my chair. How'd Hillard know some kid wouldn't sneak in at recess and just pop the littlest pumpkin on the scale?

He went on to explain that we were also to guess the circumference and diameter of the pumpkins. It was okay to use our hands or arms to estimate, but we couldn't bring a ruler to the counter. And last, we were to guess the number of seeds each pumpkin held.

On Friday, which was Halloween, Mr. Hillard would weigh and measure the circumference of the pumpkins. Then we could cut them open, measure the diameter, and count the seeds. That would be a gooshy mess, I thought.

Mr. Hillard ended by asking if there were any questions. There weren't. I tipped my chair back down. It was almost recess and time to get our desks cleared off. When Kathy passed out the playground equipment, I took a basketball.

Pete and I played one-on-one until the loud-mouthed kid and his friend joined us. The loud-mouthed kid kept shooting fifteen feet from the basket and his friend kept complaining, "Why do you try those stupid shots?"

After about ten minutes I was sweating, so I tossed my jacket on the edge of the court. Pete and I were ahead twelve to three when the bell ending recess rang. We smacked our hands together before I picked up my jacket and started toward the classrooms.

I was halfway there when a younger kid pulled on

21

my arm. He looked like he might be in fourth grade. "Your last name Johnson?" he asked.

"Ya," I said.

"Then this must be your letter."

He watched me closely while I took the folded envelope from him and looked at it. "Oh, it probably fell out of my pocket," I said. "Thanks."

"From your dad?" The kid was still watching me closely.

"Yes," I told him.

"He has an interesting address," the kid said.

"So?" I turned away from him and went into the school building.

After school Grace didn't stop to change her hair at the bus stop. "Mad at your mom?" I asked.

"No," she said. "This is Tuesday and Mom goes to a meeting on Tuesday. She won't be home until five."

"What are you going to do?"

"Nothing. Nobody's home." We were walking along side by side and she suddenly stopped. "How about your tree house? What's it like inside?"

I gave her a cautious sidewise glance. "How'd you know about my tree house?"

"I saw you build it last Sunday. You put it right across from my bedroom window."

"My mistake."

"No, it isn't," she said indignantly. "Nobody else has an upstairs room by your tree and I'm not going to tell anyone."

We started walking along again. The only thing on

22

TV in the afternoon is cartoons for babies and dumb talk shows. Mom leaves for work at two and never gets back from the restaurant until after ten. I don't like my own company that much.

"As long as you already know about it," I told Grace, "you might as well come on up and see it."

"Okay," she agreed. "I'll come over right after I change my clothes."

I got ready for Grace's visit by getting my checkerboard out of my closet and a couple pillows off the couch. I set everything up on my platform and waited for Grace. She came climbing up the tree ladder in about two minutes.

"Wow, this is neat." She walked all around the circle, then leaned over the edge. "Gol, you can see right in our kitchen."

"Naw, your blinds are always closed."

"Not all the time. Only when Mom forgets to open them in the morning." She turned and stared up at the roofing paper. "This place will be nice and dry in the winter. Where'd you get the tar paper? And where'd you get all the wood? It must have cost a lot."

"I got it for free. They're building a new store down the street." I sat on one of the cushions and started putting the checkers on the board. "Come on. I'll beat you."

"You wish," she said, and sat down across from me.

"Red or black?" I asked.

"Red."

She moved and then I moved and then she moved and I moved and she moved. And then I concentrated. Beating her wasn't going to be easy.

23

She patted the floor planks while waiting for me. "You got all this neat wood from a scrap pile?"

I put my finger on one of the black pieces. "That's what I tell my mom."

"You mean you stole it?"

"What are you, *PK*? Some kind of saint?"

"No. But what about the builder? He has to pay for the wood."

"So? It isn't going to break him." I shoved my checker forward a space.

She quickly moved her piece to meet mine and then asked me, "What would you have done if the builder had driven up while you were taking his stuff?"

"Run. What do you think?" I put my finger on another piece while I planned my attack.

"Well, how would you feel if you'd bought the lumber for your tree house and some kid came in the night and stole half of it?"

"I wouldn't be dumb enough to leave it out." I gave up on the piece I had my finger on and shoved another one forward. "Your move, *PK*."

"I know it, JJ."

While she was poring over the board, I felt like getting her off my back by making a crack about what the church next to her house was doing to her head. I decided I'd better not. Since she was the only kid in the neighborhood, I'd better not make her mad.

She made her move.

I kept my mouth shut and made my move.

She picked up her red checker and hopped over three of my pieces. "King me! King me!" she crowed.

4

The Blackmailer

The fourth-grade kid tagged after me again at the end of recess. "Hey, Johnson, wait up!" he hollered.

I looked around at him, pretending to be annoyed, and then went on walking with Pete. The kid pulled on my arm. "Hey, I lost my lunch money. Can I borrow some?"

I jerked free of him. "I bring my lunch. I don't have any money."

He whirled around in front of me, making me stop for him. "Hey, I'll borrow some from my teacher. And tomorrow you can give me the money to pay her back."

"You're nuts," I said.

He nodded his head toward Pete, who was opening the door to the school building. "Johnson, you don't want anyone to find out where your dad lives."

I itched to smash the little toad in his gut, but he only came up to my nose. "How come you know so much about that address?" I asked him before I shoved him out of the way and went for the building.

"Don't forget to bring the money tomorrow," he called after me.

We had art after recess. Mr. Hillard passed out big sheets of drawing paper, put a record on, and told us to draw pictures of how the music made us feel. After we were settled down, he settled down at his desk with his book.

I didn't know about the music, but I knew how I felt about that fourth-grade blackmailer. I took red and black crayons out of my box and slashed them across my paper. The trouble was that if I hit the kid, I'd be called a bully, and how could I explain that? If I didn't cough up some money, the little nark would spread it around that my dad was in prison. Either way I'd be dead in this school.

I picked up a yellow-green crayon and made circles over the black slashes. The thing to do was to catch the kid after school and off the school grounds. That way I could pound on him until he was convinced he wasn't going to get any money. And he'd have to keep his mouth shut or we'd have another meeting.

When the period was almost over, Mr. Hillard got up and walked around the room to look at our work. Lucky for him he wasn't still reading his book, because Mrs. Nettle came in the door. She joined him in looking over our pictures.

She stood by Pete's and my table so long, I felt my face grow hot. "Nice drawing," she said to Pete. "Interesting!" she said to me.

What did that mean?

Soon as we got out of school, I went up by the fourth-grade section and followed the students out of their building. I spotted the little blackmailer going for one of the buses. Rats. I was hoping he'd be a walker. Now I'd have to figure out another way to shut him up.

After he sat down in his bus, he poked his finger at the window facing me. "What's that kid's name?" I asked a girl standing in the bus line.

"Edward Troller," she said. "He's mean."

I bet he was. And I noticed she called him Edward, not Ed or Eddie.

I barely made it to my bus. The driver was already revving up his engine. He wasn't too pleased when I banged on the doors, but he opened them up for me. "Next time get out here when you're supposed to," he growled.

On the way home, Grace told me she was going shopping with her mother. "What for?" I asked her.

"A present," she said.

"Today's your birthday?"

"No. My birthday isn't until next week. Today she'll buy me a guilt present."

"Okay," I said, "what's a guilt present?"

Grace looked real pleased with herself. "Well, see, my brother can worm anything he wants out of my mom. Then she worries that it will look like she favors him. So she buys me something.

"She just paid for painting his car after his girlfriend scratched it. I was there when Matt gave her the shop bill. When I asked how much it was, she just mumbled around about it being too much and wrote out a check. I put the saggy-eyed treatment on her while she handed Matt the check, so today I get a guilt present."

"You get to buy as much as the paint cost?" I wanted to know.

"No," she said. "I never get that much. But I'm going to have a birthday party. Do you want to come?"

"It depends. Will any other boys be there?"

"I'm going to ask Pete. You know Pete. He sits next to you. His parents go to our church and he's in my Sunday school class."

Hmm, I thought, that must have been the preacher going in her back door all right.

We had walked home by then and were standing in front of her house. "Well," she said. "Do you want to come to my party?"

"I guess so," I said.

It was too cold and clammy out to go up in my tree house. I got some paper and sat down at the kitchen table to write my dad. I really wanted to tell him about Edward Troller and ask him what he thought I should do.

I didn't, though. It might make my dad think he was responsible. I wrote a letter about my schoolwork and the pumpkins.

After I addressed the envelope, burning hate against Troller came up to my throat. The front of my envelope just had my dad's name, Jerry Johnson, Sr., and a box number in Monroe. The only way anyone would know it was the address of the Monroe Reformatory was if he knew somebody in there. That little rat Troller should know how bad that made you feel.

He also should know a fourth grader doesn't take on a fifth grader. But he was so slippery, I couldn't figure out how to get him. Until I did, the only thing

I could think up to do was to split before recess was over.

       I tossed the ball to Pete when I thought the bell was about to ring. "I gotta take a leak," I said.

"Get a pass from the playground teacher first," he told me, "or you'll get in trouble."

I swiveled my head around. "Where is she?"

"In the covered area," Marvin said. Marvin is the name of the loudmouthed kid. As soon as I'd heard him called that, I snickered to myself. No wonder he was always trying to be a big shot.

The playground teacher was chewing out two girls for fighting over a jump rope. While I waited for her to notice me, I jiggled up and down a couple times to make it look like I really had to go. I'm a pretty good actor.

"What do you want?" she asked me after the girls had slunk away.

"I have to go to the can . . . a . . . bathroom."

"Recess is almost over," she said. "Can't you wait to get a pass from your teacher?"

I jiggled once more. "No. I don't think so."

Frowning, she gave me a wooden clothespin with the words BOYS BATH inked on it. "If you don't get back out here before the bell rings, return that to your teacher."

"Okay," I agreed, and dashed for the school building. I didn't know where Troller was, but I wasn't giving him a chance to spot me.

The bell hadn't rung by the time I got out of the can,

so I strolled on down to our classroom. Just as I got to the door, Mrs. Nettle clamped a hand on my shoulder. "How come you're in the halls, Jerry?"

I held up the clothespin. "I had to go to the bathroom and I figured recess was about over so I might as well wait in the room."

She took the clothespin from me while she gave me a cool stare that traveled right to my bones. "If you have an emergency and need to come in at recess, you go right back out after you're through. Do you understand that?"

"Yes. Yes, but I didn't even know you had to get a pass until the kids out there told me." I hadn't finished explaining before she turned me firmly around and steered me toward the outside doors.

Lucky for me, the bell rang just as I got to the bottom step. I went back through the doors, into Hillard's room, and gave each pumpkin a pat on the way to my seat.

5

The Prisoner's Kid

When I got home from school my mom was sitting on the couch with her bare feet propped up on the coffee table. As I walked past her, I kicked at the high-heeled shoes that were on the floor. "What do you wear these things for anyway?"

She concentrated on rubbing her ankles. "I have to look good at work."

"You think those wiggly worms crawling up your legs make you look good?" I went in the kitchen to get myself a sandwich. When I came back in the living room, Mom was still rubbing away. The purple veins bulging out of her white flesh made me shiver. "Why don't you get some low-heeled shoes?"

"Because, I told you, I have to dress nice at work. And anyway, my legs are already a mess."

"So it's intelligent to make them worse?" I switched on the TV and flipped through the channels. There were commercials on all of them, except one. And that one had a woman sitting on a stool yammering about some gorgeous guy in a soap opera.

I turned off the TV and dropped on the couch

beside Mom. "Listen, I saw on a science show that doctors can shoot some stuff in your veins that make them sink back down to normal."

She stopped stroking her legs to eye my half-eaten tuna sandwich. "Gimme a bite," she said.

I gave her a bite.

"So," I asked her. "Why don't you get those things pricked?"

"Because my tips barely cover the rent. We can't live on my waitress salary, you know."

I finished the last of the sandwich, wiped my mouth with the back of my hand, and then wiped my hand on my jeans. "Maybe Dad will send us more money from his new job."

"Maybe," she said.

"Listen, tomorrow's Halloween. Do you think you could stuff your feet into my old boots and hobble out to the car to get me some vampire teeth?"

She poked her head toward me. "Vampire teeth?"

"Well, I gotta have something to go trick-or-treating in. That's the cheapest thing I can think of."

"And I'm going to wear boys' boots to the store?"

"Who can tell?" I gave her my best grin, took her arm, and pulled. "Come on. You probably have to get some food for dinner, anyway."

"Great, I go shopping on my day off." She grumbled some more, but she got up from the couch and took me to the store.

There was a whole section of Halloween stuff at Safeway. I asked Mom for two dollars and suggested she do her grocery shopping while I picked out the teeth. There were some ugly ones for a dollar fifty-nine. I went through the quick checkout line by myself. I was hoping to pocket enough change to keep Troller shut up until I could pound him.

While I waited in the car for my mom, I spotted a pile of pumpkins in a bin outside of Safeway. Hillard's contest was the next day. I was about to get out of the car and weigh some of the pumpkins when Mom hurried out the door. She wanted to split right away, so I figured I'd just missed my chance.

I had, too. My guesses were way out. Grace's weren't, though. When Mr. Hillard weighed the smallest pumpkin, Grace's estimate was off by only three ounces. She won the prize to skip four assignments in any subject she wanted. Lucky her.

"How'd you do it?" I asked her while we were playing basketball in my backyard after school.

"Hillard said we could use our hands. So I stretched my fingers around the pumpkins. My middle fingers met at the center of the smallest one. Then I got Matt to drive me to a pumpkin patch and I measured and measured until I found a pumpkin that my middle fingers went around and I weighed it. Simple." And with that explanation done, she stopped dribbling, shot for a basket, and made it. Simple.

"You're a pretty good basketball player for a girl," I told her while I bounced the ball I'd caught off the backboard.

That brought her to a sudden halt. She stopped waving her arms to guard me and placed her hands on her hips. "Whatta you mean 'for a girl'?"

"Well, well." I bounced the ball a couple more times. "Well, girls are usually shorter than guys."

She kept her hands on her hips. "You're not much taller than I am."

"Ya, that's right." I tried grinning at her. I didn't want to get started on this with Grace. I'd had enough of it from my mom. "Hey, how about knocking off for a while and getting something to eat. We have a whole sack of apples from the Brethren House."

"You go get a couple of them," she said. "I'll wait out here."

This was the first time Grace had come over when her mother was home. While I got the apples out of the fridge, I wondered if her mother had told her not to come in my house. Since my mom wasn't around, I guess it was reasonable for Grace to be told to stay outside, but it left me with a funny feeling.

We sat on the ground beneath the basketball hoop while we ate our apples. "These are good," Grace said. "Not all mushy."

"Ya," I agreed. "They're probably from some church lady's yard."

She looked at me surprised. "Church lady?"

"I suppose so." I shrugged. "They're the ones who give the stuff to the Brethren House."

Grace still looked bewildered.

"The Brethren House. Don't you know the Brethren House?"

"No." She shook her head. "But my dad probably does."

"Probably."

Grace threw her apple core in the bushes beside the garage. "I've got a problem about the party," she said. "My mom is super straight."

"I guessed."

"Ya, well, she might think we should give a blessing before we eat the cake and ice cream and maybe the kids at the party will think it's dumb."

"Oh, that's no big problem." I tossed my apple core into the bushes too. "I'll think of a funny prayer and say it before your mom can start anything."

Grace frowned thoughtfully at the ground. "That'd do it, but . . . but it can't be so funny it'll make my mom mad."

"No, no, it'll just be saying grace for giving Grace a bountiful cake or something. Better than that, though." I really couldn't think of anything good at the moment. I hoped I would later, because Grace had stopped looking at the ground and was smiling at me. She has pretty white teeth and dark blue eyes, and her smile sort of threw me. I reached out for the basketball and concentrated on twirling it in my hand. "Your mom's real religious?"

"Sure," Grace said. "My dad's a minister, you know."

The ball dropped from my hand as the man from the church coming in her back door flashed in my mind. "Preacher's kid! That's what you are. A preacher's kid!"

"Of course. What did you think?" She stared at me like I was crazy. "What did you think PK meant?"

I stared back at her with my mouth open until her mom yelling "Gracie! Gracie!" split the air a few seconds later.

Grace stood up to leave.

35

"Gracie!" her mom hollered. "It's time to set the table."

"I gotta go," Grace said. "I'll meet you in front of my house after dinner, okay?"

I just sat there.

"We're going trick-or-treating like we planned, aren't we?"

I nodded at my feet and she left.

The last thing I wanted to do was go trick-or-treating with her. And I sure wasn't going to her party. What if her mom found out about my dad? Chances are she would, too.

When Troller had followed me at the end of recess that day, I'd flipped him a quarter. "Hey, this isn't going to do it, Johnson," he had yelled after me. And I knew it wouldn't.

I also knew I wasn't going to figure out how to catch him off the school grounds while I sat listening to my stomach growl. I dragged myself up and went in the house to open a can of soup. I ate in front of the TV, worrying about Troller and worrying about Grace.

There really wasn't any way I could get out of going with Grace after dinner. She knew I wasn't sick. She knew I didn't have anybody else to go with. And we'd talked about doing Halloween together on the way home from school.

After I'd washed my soup bowl, I pulled on an old ski cap and stuck the vampire teeth in my mouth. I'd meant to blacken some cotton with ink and stick it on my face, but I didn't feel like doing that anymore.

I went over to Grace's and stood in her yard until

she came out. "I didn't know you were here already," she said. "Why didn't you knock?"

I didn't answer her. She had on a black cape and a pointed hat and a long putty chin. She was carrying a shopping bag with a witch's picture on it. I was just carrying an old grocery sack.

After we'd come off the porch of the third house with three more candy bars, she asked me, "What's the matter with you, anyway?"

"Nothing," I said.

"Yes, there is!"

I walked silently down the street. What could I say?

She stopped under the streetlight on the corner and dragged on my shoulder. "Come on. What's the matter?"

"What makes you think anything's the matter?"

"Well, you're drooling around your teeth. . . ."

I turned my face away and wiped my mouth off with my jacket sleeve.

"No, no," she laughed. "That isn't it. I know you're not having a good time because you aren't grinning your usual pumpkin grin."

"How can I with these vampire teeth?" I wiped my mouth again. Every time I talked I drooled. I took the stupid teeth out. "There, now do I look happy?"

"No," she said.

I crossed the street fast, while she trotted after me. "Let's try the houses on this side," I suggested.

"No!" She grabbed on my jacket again. "We're supposed to be friends. Or at least I thought we were friends. I told you when I was worried about saying grace at my party."

"I can't go to your party," I blurted out.

"You can't go to my party? Why not?"

I just stood there.

"Why—can't—you?" She drew the words out slowly, leaning straight into my face.

"Be—cause," I said just as slowly, "I'm the wrong kind of PK. I'm a prisoner's kid."

Smoke
the Little Toad

I tried to see Grace's expression through the dark of the night, but she was no longer leaning into my face. I waited uneasily for her to say something. She was the only friend I had and I'd probably blown it.

"I think you're neat," she said. "And you can't help what your dad does." She paused for a minute. "I wouldn't spread it around, though. Some kids like a chance to put you down."

I barked out a laugh. "That's for sure."

She started walking down the sidewalk, and this time I followed her. "Have you told anybody else?" she asked.

"Troller knows."

"Troller," she said. "Who's Troller?"

And so I explained about Edward Troller and his blackmailing and how I didn't have any money because my mom was just a waitress. And how I'd looked up Troller in the phone book, but I didn't know how to get to his address. I ended by telling Grace that there was no way I could keep away from Troller at recess.

39

"Yes, there is," she said. "Just get a library pass instead of a basketball and go and read in the library."

"Boring."

"Sure, but it'll work until we can figure out what to do about Edward Troller."

"I'd like to smoke the little toad."

"I'd like to see him."

"Just look for the rattiest kid in the fourth grade."

Grace giggled. "Come on. This house is all lit up. Let's get some more stuff."

The lady in the lit-up house gave us pink popcorn balls, which I hate. The next house gave us packages of sugarless gum, which is okay. The people at the end of the block popped handfuls of foil-wrapped chocolate kisses in our bags. "Aw right!" I said.

"We'd better start home," Grace said. "My mom told me to be back in an hour."

"You can't get much in an hour in this neighborhood."

"I know, but you know my mom. Or you will know her when you come to my party next Wednesday, right?"

"Maybe," I said.

"No maybes!" She waited until we'd crossed the street again before she asked, "What'd your dad do, anyway?"

"He parted out cars."

"How do you do that?"

"You take the engine or the tires or the headlights or whatever off the car and sell them."

She seemed to think that over while we walked

along. When we were almost to my house, she said, "But where did he get the cars?"

"He stole them." I could almost feel the shock go through her. She sure was a preacher's kid. "I'll see, ya, PK," I said, and took off across my lawn.

She came after me and yanked on the back of my jacket. "You *are* coming to my party."

I kept facing away from her. "Are you sure you want me? What about your mom?"

"I'm sure I want you. And what my mom doesn't know won't hurt her." And with that, Grace ran across the driveway to her house.

I watched her go. It was nice that she still wanted to be my friend, but I figured it would only last until her mom found out where my dad was. I shivered just imagining the horror on Mrs. Elliott's face.

At school I went to the library during the morning recess. Mr. Folsom, the librarian, is pretty cool. He helped me find some interesting books on stars. I looked for a picture of the Big Dipper and the Little Dipper first. And then I followed the tip of the Big Dipper's cup to the North Star. The North Star and my dad. I sat in the hard library chair and wondered how long it would be before he got a parole.

At lunch recess I went out and played basketball with Pete. The fourth graders have their lunch earlier than the fifth graders, so their noon recess ends earlier. I didn't even catch sight of Troller until Tuesday.

He had another fourth-grade kid backed against the climbing bars. The way his face was pushed close to the other kid's made me think Troller was threatening him. The kid looked scared to death. All of a sudden

41

Troller's hand shot out and his stiffened fingers jabbed the kid in the gut. The kid bent over in pain.

Before I knew what I was doing, I'd dropped the basketball and was going for Troller. Mrs. Wilson beat me to him. She wasn't the least scared of the little rat. She caught him up by the back of his neck and had him skidding toward the office before *he* knew what was happening.

I thought maybe I'd be rid of him for a while, but he was out again after lunch Wednesday. He came right up to where Pete and I were playing. "Hey, Johnson," he said, "I need to talk to you."

I kept on dribbling the ball. "Ya? What's up?"

"We gotta talk *now.*" Troller had his arms crossed over his chest.

I bounced the ball to Pete and walked to the edge of the court. "Okay, what's the big deal?"

"I'm short of money," he said.

"That's your problem," I said.

"It can be a bigger problem to you."

I shrugged. "Too bad. I don't have any money. My mom doesn't have any money."

"There are ways to get it, Johnson." He'd half closed his eyes and turned his mouth down into a sneer. He looked like a baby Rattler. If I hadn't been so worried about the whole school knowing my dad was a convict, I would have laughed at him.

Instead, I glanced over at Pete, who was shooting baskets by himself. "Hmmm," I said slowly. "Maybe you're right. Tell me how to get to your house and I might be able to meet you somewhere tonight."

"No way. You wouldn't like my big brother." The

42

bell rang, ending the fourth-grade recess. He backed up a few steps. "You bring me some bills tomorrow."

"We'll see," I said and left him to catch the ball Pete tossed me.

When our bell rang, Pete and I walked back to the classroom together. Pete's thin and real blond. You can barely see his eyebrows. He has long legs, too, and I have to move along to keep up with him.

He was quiet all the way to Hillard's door, and then he burst out, "I wouldn't have much to do with Troller if I were you."

Pete went into the room ahead of me. "What's wrong with Troller?" I asked, as if I didn't know.

Pete dumped the basketball in the wooden box in the corner before he answered. "His brother's been in the reformatory."

"So?"

"Well, Troller's really a wienie, but he likes to pretend he's part of the Mafia."

"That's for sure." My laugh sounded phony even to me.

On the way home from school, I didn't get to think much more about Troller, because Grace kept babbling about her party. "Pete's coming and Nicky and Mari are coming and Mom ordered a big sheet cake from Albertson's and she's got stuff for the flour game—"

"Flower game? You think Pete will like a game with flowers?"

"Flour. Flour. Like in pancakes, stupid."

"Oh."

I'd gotten mixed up over Grace's present, too. Mom had said she'd pick up something at the drugstore on the way back from her Sunday visit with Dad. "Maybe some toilet water," she said.

"Toilet water!" I yelled. "You think Grace will like toilet water?"

"Calm down," Mom told me. "Toilet water is the same as cologne. They're perfume."

Sure. Sounds just like perfume.

Mom bought tissue paper and pink ribbon, too. She showed me how to pull the ribbon over the sharp edge of the scissors to make it curl. I hate pink and I wasn't going to make any curls. I waited until just before the party to wrap Grace's present.

While I tied the ribbon into a shoestring bow, I tried to think of something to say before we ate the cake and ice cream. Everything I could think of sounded dumb. While I ran water over my comb in the bathroom and combed my hair, I still tried to think of something. The problem was, the song Dad sang to me on my sixth birthday kept getting in the way.

Happy birthday to you
You live in a zoo
You look like a monkey
And smell like one too.

My first-grade friends had laughed until they fell out of their chairs. I could never be as funny as my dad.

7

Party Down

For girls came to Grace's party and only two guys. There wasn't much to do until everyone got there. Pete and I just stood around listening to Grace squeal every time somebody handed her a present. Grace acts a lot sappier in her house than she does at mine.

After Mari, the last girl, dumped her present on Grace, Mrs. Elliott herded us all into the kitchen. She lined us up in front of a flat pan that was sitting on the counter. Beside the pan was a spatula. Inside the pan was a big pile of flour. On top of the pile was a red candy heart.

Reverend Elliott explained that the point of the game was to scoop away the flour without letting the candy heart fall off the top. We all managed to do this the first time around. The second time, though, the red heart dropped off when Mari cut into the flour. That put her out of the game, but first she had to pick up the candy with her mouth. She came out of the pan with white flour hanging from her nose, eyelashes, and eyebrows.

Reverend Elliott put another heart on the pile.

Nicky, who was ahead of me, sliced away a teeny bit of flour. I took a good look at the mound when it was my turn. I figured if I cut off most of the left side, Pete would have to cut on the right, where the flour was sure to cave in.

It did, too. After Pete ducked for the red heart, he came up with it in his teeth all right, but then he sneezed and the candy and flour flew out of his mouth. I barely jumped out of his way in time.

At the end of the game there was just me and Grace's cousin Nicky in line. Nicky was pretty cagy about scooping a couple grains of flour away from the pile that was left. I tried to do the same, but the candy heart slipped to the side and sank out of sight.

That meant I had to bury my whole mouth into the pan to get the candy. When I came up, Pete pointed to my face and bent over laughing. That made me laugh, too, which was a mistake. I inhaled and choked on the flour.

Each time I tried to get a breath, more flour from my face went down my windpipe. My lungs burned, tears sprung from my eyes, and I thought I was going to suffocate. I had my hands wrapped around my throat and my heart was thumping in panic, when Reverend Elliott whacked me on the back.

Flour sprayed from my mouth and all over Mrs. Elliott, who was standing in front of me. She brushed frantically at her dress, but the flour was mixed with my spit and it stuck. Reverend Elliott steered me into the bathroom while Mrs. Elliott went upstairs to change her cothes.

After I'd washed and dried my face and blown my

nose on a wad of toilet paper, I leaned against the counter. "I think I ruined your wife's best dress."

"No, no," Reverend Elliott told me. "Flour washes out easily. No problem. The important thing is, how do you feel now?"

"Okay, I guess."

"Good!" He put his arm around my shoulders. "Let's go outside and play a little water wienie."

Water wienie. That was more my style. You play water wienie with pieces of light brown hose. Like the kind a doctor uses to make your vein pop out so he can siphon off your blood.

You tie a knot in one end and fill the other end with water, which stretches out the tube to about one and a half feet. Then you put an empty ballpoint-pen case in the open end. You keep your finger over the pen until you want to squirt the water.

By the time we'd gotten the hoses all filled on the faucet by the side of Grace's house, everybody's shoes were wet. The girls tried to dry theirs by stamping their feet in the grass. Pete and I just squished around. This was nothing compared to the soaking that came later.

The game started off tame enough. Reverend Elliott put a bucket on a stand in the front yard. We were supposed to take turns trying to squirt it off.

Grace knocked down the bucket first. Then Pete did. Then Lynnette did. Reverend Elliott went in the house before Mari's turn. She didn't knock down the bucket, but after she finished her shot, she just "accidentally" kept her finger off the end of the pen as she turned around. I got it right in the face.

"Just wait," I told her when she passed me to go to the end of the line.

She shrugged and grinned. She didn't care. She's the rowdiest girl in our room.

On my turn, I knocked the bucket down and then whirled around Rambo-like and gave it to Mari all down her front. Grace came to Mari's rescue and Pete backed me up. Then all the girls were on Pete and me, so we dived behind the bucket stand.

While we tried to take short squirts at each of the girls, Mari and Grace raced behind the stand and got us down our backs. Pete and I stood up and let them have it straight on.

Grace's ribbon was hanging down her wet hair and her party dress was a mess by the time Mrs. Elliott hurried out the front door. "Gracie! Just look at yourself!"

"Oh, hi, Mom," Grace said.

End of water wienie. Pete and I pulled the pen cases out of our hoses and concentrated on the water dribbling on the ground. Reverend Elliott followed his wife down the front steps. "It's pretty cold out here. Maybe you all better come in and dry off. And have a little birthday cake. How about it, guys?"

"Sure," Pete and I said together.

Mrs. Elliott seated Pete and me on opposite sides of the party table. While she lit the candles on the cake, Pete took his fork in his fist and made little, secret, jabbing motions toward the balloons over our heads. I tried not to laugh.

Grace blew out the eleven candles on the cake, and then Mrs. Elliott cut it into squares and put it on our plates. Reverend Elliott scooped out the ice cream, giving us a choice between raspberry and vanilla. I took raspberry and Pete took both.

When her parents had almost gotten around the table, I caught Grace staring intently at me. I nodded at her. She sat back in her chair.

Just as her dad closed the ice cream cartons and her mother took in a breath to speak, I raised both my hands in the air. "We will now give thanks." I swooped my hands down, directing every head to follow.

"Dear Lord, we thank thee for this food so neat." I swooped up my hands, directing every head to rise. "And now, gang. Let's eat!"

Reverend Elliott chuckled, Pete jammed his fork into his cake, and Grace shot me a blue-eyed cheer. The cold ice cream couldn't chill the warm feeling that spread through my insides. It lasted until my plate was clean and all through the opening of presents.

Mrs. Elliott thought my gift of "toilet water" was sweet. She said "Tea Rose" was her favorite scent. Grace sprayed it on herself and all over Nicky, Kris, Mari, and Lynnette. Pete and I ducked.

Mrs. McCartney, Pete's mom, was the first parent to arrive. She told him to thank Grace and Mrs. Elliott for inviting him. Before I went out the door, I thanked them too. I was still feeling so good I jumped the bushes at the edge of my yard.

8

The Swirly

Before recess on Thursday I raised my hand for a library pass. Pete looked disgusted. "Not again!"

"Just for today," I told him. "I gotta look up something."

He caught up with two other guys after we left the room. I hurried on to the library knowing I had to get Troller fast. Pete would find somebody else to play basketball with if I wasn't around.

Mr. Folsom helped me find a map of Snohomish. There was only one Troller in the county phone book and I'd written the address on a piece of paper. I traced my finger over all the streets of the town, but Troller's wasn't anywhere.

I returned the map to Mr. Folsom, held out my paper, and asked him if he knew where the house was located. "I think it's over toward Mill Creek," he said.

"But that's out of town. A kid who lived way over there wouldn't be going to this school, would he?"

"He might. Sometimes schools take students from out of the district."

I looked up into Mr. Folsom's bearded face. "Why?"

"Well, if they need a special program that their district can't provide."

"That's all?" I asked.

Mr. Folsom squinted his eyes in thought. He was sitting on his stool behind the checkout counter. I put my elbow on the counter and kept my eyes on his eyes. "Sometimes," Mr. Folsom said, "a student has problems in his home school and his parents or the principal might think he'd be better off with a fresh start in a new place."

"But . . . but then would he ride the school bus? How would he get to his house?"

"He could ride the school bus to a Metro bus stop or his parents could pick him up at the end of the line."

I heaved a big sigh. That's probably what was happening to Troller all right. I thanked Mr. Folsom for his help and went back to my seat and slouched in it until the bell rang, ending recess.

I spent the next hour in Hillard's class staring at a ditto that was titled TWENTY-NINE WAYS TO DO A BOOK REPORT. I could "Act out part of the book" or "Make a crossword puzzle from all the characters in the book" or "Do a TV commercial to sell the book" or "Make a poster to advertise the book" or . . .

I drew a head on the margin of the ditto. I made a long, pointy nose coming down from the forehead. Just like Troller. He even looked like a rat.

The thing to do was to call the Metro bus station and find out which bus would take me by Troller's street. Then I'd have to wait around until I saw Troller come out of his house. That might take a long time. If I started early Saturday morning before Mom got up to ask a lot of questions about where I was going . . .

There were two light taps on my head. "Earth to Jerry! Earth to Jerry!"

I looked up to see Mari flash me a grin as she walked by my seat on her way to the wastebasket. I'd been spacing out all right. Most of the kids in the room had their colored markers or their scissors on their desks.

I opened my library book. I decided I might as well do number eleven. "Write a different ending to the story."

At the noon recess I took a basketball even though Troller would hassle me for sure. Pete and I were playing with two other kids when he did. "Hey, Johnson!" he hollered. "What does your dad do for a living?"

"He's an exterminator," I hollered back. "So you better watch it."

Troller stepped closer to the court. "Hey, Johnson, where's your dad live?"

I bounced the ball to Pete and moved over to Troller. "Cool it, loudmouth, or you'll spoil your racket. Everything's taken care of. You'll get yours by Monday."

"It better be bills," he warned me.

"It'll be good," I said.

He gave me a suspicious look before he closed his mouth over his little yellow teeth and took off for the other side of the playground.

53

On our walk home from the bus stop, Grace asked me how come I'd been out to recess. "Not afraid of Troller anymore?"

"I've never been *afraid* of him," I told her. "I'm just worried about his mouth."

"Is your mother going to the school open house Friday night?"

"Yep," I said. "She's working today and taking tomorrow off."

"Well, then, why don't you have her talk to Mrs. Nettle while she's there. Mrs. Nettle can shut Troller up."

I picked up a beer can from under a bush and heaved it across the street. "Sure, until he got one of his friends to spread the news."

"Mrs. Nettle could warn him not to do that."

"Don't be dumb, PK. How would she know if he did? Even a fourth grader would have better sense than to tell on Troller."

Grace stopped in front of her house, undid her hair, and plopped her ribbon on top of her head. I guess she forgot to change it at the bus stop. As she put her extra bobby pin in her purse, she said, "What are you going to do, then?"

"I'm going to ride the Metro out to his house on Saturday and beat on his mouth until he can't say 'uncle.'"

Grace hesitated before going in her gate. I could see this wasn't her idea of solving a problem. But, then, she didn't know Troller. "See ya, PK," I said, and went on to my house.

After dinner on Friday, Mom swished into the living room and whirled around in front of me. "Will I do?" she asked.

My mom's a bottle blonde with brown eyes like mine. She's kinda pretty, or is if she remembers to wear her glasses when she puts on makeup.

She leaned her head toward me. "Well?"

"You look fine, except . . . Why don't you take some of that red stuff off your cheeks?"

"Do I have too much blush on?" She hurried into the bathroom.

I called after her. "And put on your glasses so you can see what you're doing."

When she came back, she looked all right. She said I did too. I was wearing a white shirt, jeans, and my high-tops, which she'd cleaned with bleach. We went off in the car to Silver King's open house.

When we got within three blocks of the school, people were already jammed up trying to find parking places. "Take a left," I told Mom, "and we'll get out of this mess."

"No," she said, "I'm going in the teachers' parking lot. There might be an empty space."

She was right. There was one at the tail end of the lot. It was a good thing, because her old Camaro doesn't fit into tight places. It guzzles gas, too, but it's the only car my dad paid for. At least, I think he did, because he put it in Mom's name.

Inside the door of the school I pulled on her arm. "Let's go to the library first. I want you to meet a neat guy."

There were a couple of parents talking to Mr. Folsom. I showed Mom the astronomy books in the science section while we waited for him. As soon as he was rid of the parents, Mr. Folsom came up and introduced himself. He put his hand on my shoulder and said to Mom, "You have a nice boy here."

"I like him," she said.

"Are you interested in stars too?" he asked.

Mom shook her head. "No, Jerry gets that from his dad."

Mr. Folsom smiled and nodded, but he didn't ask if my dad was at the open house or anything. I wondered if he knew where he was.

On the way to my classroom I asked Mom, "Do you think teachers get to see a kid's records?"

"I think so," she said. "But I don't think people like Mr. Folsom hold that against you. It'd probably just make him want to help you."

Helping might be all right, but I didn't want anybody feeling sorry for me.

Grace and her parents were inside Mr. Hillard's room looking at the students' work on the wall. Wouldn't you know, my black and red slashes were up there with the other drawings. "Whatever made you draw that ugly thing?" Mom asked.

"Troller," I said.

"Who's Troller?"

"It doesn't matter. Let's go find my seat. Mr. Hillard said he gives a speech to the parents."

Before we sat down, Grace came over and introduced her parents to Mom. It always surprises me that Reverend Elliott has a long, black mustache. And he's huge. After they left, Mom whispered to me, "He looks like Fu Manchu."

I nodded. Weird preacher.

Mr. Hillard started his speech by telling the parents what a fine group of students we were and what a good learning experience we'd all had so far this year. Then he went on to the curriculum: reading, math, science, social studies, and language arts. He'd gone through six of the eight learning objectives in math when I began to numb out.

I shifted in my seat, looked at the wall, stared out the open classroom door . . . Zowee! I came to attention. Down the hall came Troller, a big, fat man, a blond woman in a zebra-striped coat, and a little girl.

The girl had a hold of the man's hand and was skipping ahead of him. The woman was trying not to stumble over the little girl. Troller was sort of lagging behind those three like he wanted to escape the whole scene.

After the family had moved out of sight, I kept watch on the hall. Sure enough, before Hillard got through the five science objectives, Troller came strolling back. "I gotta go to the can," I whispered to Mom and slipped from my seat and out the classroom door.

I ran silently down the hall until I caught up with Troller. He whirled around when I tapped him on the arm. I smiled. "Expecting trouble?"

"What do you want, Johnson?"

57

"I got something for you," I said, still smiling.

He was standing with his feet planted wide apart. He reached out his hand. "Well, give it to me."

"Naw, we gotta get out of sight. Come on down the hall a ways." I went ahead. He followed me slowly, suspiciously.

As soon as he was beside the entrance to the boys' bathroom, I grabbed the front of his shirt, twisted it hard, and shoved him through the door. I pulled him across the floor and, with all my strength, hammered him against the stall wall. His head bounced like a basketball.

"So, you're going to tell everybody about my dad, huh?"

"No, no, no. You got it wrong. I just needed some money. I owed some guys. No, no." He tried to pull away, but he's a wienie, just like Pete said.

I banged him some more until snot ran down his upper lip and he was blubbering, "I won't tell anyone. Honest. Honest."

"You're right, you won't." I kicked open a stall door, kicked up the lid to the toilet, forced Troller's head into the bowl, and pushed the flush lever with my foot. "And here's a little swirly to help you remember."

He glugged in the water, his arms and legs waving around like a starfish. His black hair fanned out and then plastered against his head as the bowl emptied. I pulled him up and shoved him out against the sinks. "Listen, if I hear one peep around this school about my dad, this is nothing to what you're going to get."

"But . . . but . . . but what if some other kid finds out and tells?"

"Too bad for you, because you're the one I'm going to pound."

After I'd let him go and he'd torn out the door, I washed my hands, combed my hair, and smiled at myself in the mirror. That would be the end of my problem with Troller, I was sure.

9

Mrs. Nettle's Office

Hillard was winding up the objectives in language arts when I slipped back in my seat beside Mom. She rolled her eyes at me, meaning she was bored out of her skull. Pete's mom must have jabbed her husband with her elbow, because his head snapped upright after Mr. Hillard folded his notes.

Hillard asked if there were any questions, but no parent there was dumb enough to ask one. He said the parents who had other children in school could go on to their classrooms. And coffee and donuts were being served in the library.

Mom and I headed for the library. She went for the coffee at the end of the table. I bellied up to the middle of the table where the donuts were stacked. I was deciding between one with chocolate frosting and one with white frosting sprinkled with coconut, when Mr. Troller's angry red face leaned down into mine. "You're Johnson, right?"

My first thought was to make a run for it, but his meaty hand clamped on my neck. So instead I mumbled, "Yes, sir."

He yanked me out of the hungry crowd and headed me for the door. "I think you have some explaining to do to the principal."

Edward Troller was waiting for us in the hall, his wet hair hanging in points around his head. A revengeful smirk crossed his face before he dropped his expression back to injured innocence. What a phony.

Mr. Troller had marched me halfway to Mrs. Nettle's office when we passed the Elliotts. Grace's blue eyes were wide with horror and she was yanking on her dad's sleeve to get his attention. After that I heard Mom's heels clacking behind us. "Just a minute!" she called out. "What is going on?"

Mr. Troller turned around. Keeping a firm grip on my neck, he asked her, "This your boy?"

"Yes, he is," Mom said. "And what do you think you're doing with him?"

"He's been hazing my kid and I'm putting a stop to it. That's what I'm doing."

She stood right up close to that fat, old man. "And when was Jerry supposed to have done this?"

"About fifteen minutes ago."

"He's been with me this evening."

"Not the whole time, he hasn't." He nodded down at her. "You'd better come along and learn something about your boy."

"I will, but first let go of my son."

Mr. Troller hesitated. I don't think he liked minding Mom. She kept her ground, though, so he dropped his hand from my neck, planted it on my back, and pushed me to the office.

Mrs. Nettle was sitting behind her desk. She was

wearing a dark blue blouse with a ruffled collar. Blue earrings dangled below her gray hair. I'd never seen her dressed so fancy.

Mrs. Troller and her little daughter were sitting in chairs in front of Mrs. Nettle. Mrs. Troller still had on her fake fur coat. Mr. Troller brought up two more chairs to the desk. Edward dragged up a couple more.

When we were all seated in a half circle, with Mr. Troller on one side of me and my mom on the other, Mrs. Nettle began, "Open house really isn't the time to . . ."

Mr. Troller's beefy jaw shot out. "All I'm asking for is the same kind of treatment you give everyone else. You're fast enough to call me down here when Eddie pokes a finger at a kid."

Pokes a *finger*? I thought. He means spikes a kid in the gut with *five stiff* fingers.

Mrs. Nettle looked down at her hands a minute, took in a breath, and put on her stern face. "All right, Edward, do you want to tell me what happened this evening?"

"Well," Edward said in a soft little voice I'd never heard him use before, "I was walking down the hall to the bathroom when this kid comes along and knocks me through the door. And then he takes me and bangs me against the wall. And after that he sticks my head in the toilet and flushes it. He wouldn't let me up and I thought I was going to drown. And then he finally let me go and I ran to my dad."

"And this 'kid' is?" Mrs. Nettle asked.

"Him." Edward flipped his thumb toward me. "Johnson."

63

"You and Jerry know each other?"

"No, I don't know him. He just grabbed me in the hall and threw me . . ."

"But you know his name," Mrs. Nettle said.

"Well, sure. I heard guys call him that on the playground."

"Way over from the fourth-grade side?"

"I don't know. I . . ." Edward was fogetting to use his little helpless voice. "Maybe I heard the guys call him that when we were all going in."

Mrs. Nettle eyed Edward a minute and then turned to me. "Did you take Edward in the bathroom and knock him against the wall and put his head in the toilet?"

I swallowed before I answered yes. I could feel my mom stiffen beside me.

"Why?" Mrs. Nettle asked.

"Because he was going to tell all the kids that my dad's in the reformatory if I didn't . . ."

"No way!" Edward said loudly. "I seen you around school, but I never seen your dad."

"How could Eddie know this boy's dad?" Mr. Troller growled. "We don't live here. The boy admits he was hazing Eddie. It don't make no difference what story he makes up. He's twice as big as Eddie."

I'm dead, I thought to myself. I'm dead.

Mrs. Nettle was staring at her hands again. She seemed to do that a lot around Mr. Troller. After he finished talking, she looked up at me. "Why do you think Edward knows where your father is?"

"Because I dropped . . ." My voice came out in squeaks. I cleared my throat to start over. "While I was playing basketball, I left my jacket on the playground. A letter from my dad dropped . . ." My voice was still squeaky. You're not dead yet, I tried to tell myself. And don't cry!

Mom put a hand on my shoulder. Before I went on, I took in a long, shaky breath. "The letter dropped out of my pocket and Edward found it. He knew the address on the envelope and said if I didn't give him money he would tell everyone in school where my dad was."

"That's a big lie!" Edward said. "I never found no letter."

Mr. Troller glared down at me. I knew I was going to get creamed now. There was no way I could prove Edward blackmailed me.

But before Mr. Troller could say a word, the office door opened. When Reverend Elliott poked in his head, it was my turn to stiffen. "Mrs. Nettle," he said, "would you mind if I joined you? I realize you're having a private conference, but I think it concerns something I wanted to speak to you about this evening."

"Well . . ." Mrs. Nettle began uncertainly.

Reverend Elliott didn't wait for more of an invitation. He just came right in, picked up a chair by the wall, and poked it between Mr. Troller and me. Mr. Troller didn't have any choice but to move over. Mom and I shifted too.

When Reverend Elliott had settled down, Mrs. Nettle introduced him to the Trollers. Mr. Troller reluctantly shook the hand held out to him. The little girl said, "Hi," and Mrs. Troller smiled, trying to keep her upper lip over her crooked front teeth.

I guessed the family didn't go to the dentist much. I guessed Mrs. Troller didn't buy much hair dye, either. The ends of her hair were about the same color as my mom's, but the roots were all brown.

Reverend Elliott didn't waste any time pitching into the conference. "My daughter confided in me about the trouble between Jerry and Edward," he said. "When Edward wasn't satisfied with the little money Jerry could give him . . ."

"Where'd you get any money?" Mom snapped at me.

"What was left over from the two dollars you gave me for the vampire teeth," I said.

"Oh," she said.

"Well," Reverend Elliott went on, "Grace suggested that Jerry stay in the library during recess to avoid Edward. She felt that would give me time to talk the problem over with Mrs. Johnson and/or you, Mrs. Nettle. Unfortunately, I guess a confrontation between the boys came before . . ."

"What's the story you got from your daughter got to do with Eddie getting beat up?" Mr. Troller demanded. "How's Eddie going to threaten a kid twice his size?"

"He could if he thought he had something on the other boy," Reverend Elliott replied calmly.

"But your daughter never seen Eddie threaten this boy."

Mrs. Nettle leaned across her desk toward me. "Jerry, did anyone hear Edward threaten you?"

"Pete McCartney did," I said.

Mrs. Nettle rose from her chair. "I don't like to do

this on open house," she muttered as she left her desk and went into the outer office where the intercom was.

"If Pete McCartney is still in the building, will he please come to the office." Mrs. Nettle's voice sounded hollow coming from the empty room. I sat hoping Pete would show up and worrying about what he'd say if he did. Pete hadn't actually heard Edward threaten me.

I held my breath until a door opened. I let it out slowly as I listened to the voices.

"Pete, do you know a boy named Edward Troller?" Mrs. Nettle said.

"Sure," Pete said. "He's a fourth grader."

"Does he ever come over to the fifth-grade section at recess?"

"Ya, he comes over and bugs Jerry Johnson."

"And how does Edward do that?"

"Well, like a couple days ago, he yelled, 'Hey, Johnson, where's your dad live?' And stuff like that."

"All right, Pete, thank you for coming in. You've been helpful."

"Thank you," he said politely. Some kids won't tell a principal anything, but Pete always obeys adults.

I relaxed as I heard him close the door—until I realized I had to go to the bathroom, bad. I was twisting my hands together when Mrs. Nettle came back to her desk. She sat down and seemed to think a minute. Nobody else said a word. I didn't dare look over at the Trollers.

Mrs. Nettle dared. She looked straight at Mrs. Troller. "Has anyone in your family been in the Monroe Reformatory?"

67

"Yes," Mrs. Troller said slowly. "My stepson has."

"So, Edward," Mrs. Nettle said to him, "you recognized the return address on Jerry's envelope."

Edward shot a glance at his father, who looked like he was about to smack him off the chair. Then Edward looked at the wall, then the floor.

Mrs. Nettle rubbed her forehead. "I really don't want to call anyone else in on this."

Mr. Troller leaned back in this seat. "That won't be necessary. I'll take care of Eddie." He patted the belt denting his bulging waist. Edward followed the pat with rounded eyes, paled to a sickly green, and shriveled into his chair.

"You ain't going to turn out like your brother. I'll see to that," Mr. Troller told him.

I hate Edward, but I'd hate worse to get what I knew he was going to get.

Mrs. Nettle turned her attention to me. "Beating up on somebody is not the way to solve problems." She flicked a glance at Mr. Troller before going on. "Jerry, if you have a problem you can't solve alone, there are obviously plenty of adults to help you." She pointed first to my mom, then to Reverend Elliott, and then to herself.

I nodded. I sure wished I'd gone to the bathroom when I'd been in the can.

"I want an essay from you on my desk next Monday morning," she went on. "And I want it titled 'How I Get Help When I Need It.'"

I nodded some more.

She stood up. "Thank you for coming in, Reverend Elliott, and Mrs. Johnson."

They stood up. I stood up. Mrs. Troller stood up too. "I would like the Trollers to stay a few minutes," Mrs. Nettle added. Mrs. Troller sat down.

Out in the hall Mom said, "Why didn't you tell me . . ."

"Just a sec, Mom," I said. "I gotta go bad."

I made it to the bathroom, barely. The evening had been too scary for me.

10

View from
the Tree House

I was sitting on my front steps Saturday afternoon when Grace came over. "What are you doing?" she asked.

"Nothing," I said. "Just waiting for the mail."

She sat down beside me. "Did you get restricted?"

"Only for the weekend. I have to stay in the yard and write an essay for Mrs. Nettle."

"That's not much. What did you do to Troller, anyway?"

"I knocked him around a bit. And then I gave him a swirly."

She giggled. "I thought so. I saw this kid with soaking wet hair talking to a fat man."

"That was Troller's old man," I said.

Grace nodded. "That's what I figured when I saw him dragging you to the office."

"You narked the whole thing to your dad."

"Not exactly," she said. "My dad's supposed to help people. It isn't really narking when you tell a minister."

"What about when you tell your mom?"

Grace shook her head. "Oh, she didn't know what was going on. You can't tell my mom lots of things."

I believed that. But I didn't like worrying that Grace would blab everything I said to her dad. And I told her so.

"I do not tell everything!" She sounded real hurt. "I only told him because it was blackmail. And I knew you'd get in trouble if you had a fight with a little kid. And anyway it came out all right, didn't it?"

I shrugged. Actually, her dad had saved my skin, but I didn't want to encourage her to do any more blabbing.

Grace's brother drove into their driveway. "Matt's bringing his new girlfriend to dinner," Grace said, watching a redhead get out of his car. "I don't think she's so cute."

She sure wasn't as pretty as the girl who'd jumped on Matt's hood. This one was tall without much shape. The only thing she had going for her was a mass of kinky red hair. And that wasn't such a big deal.

"I guess I'd better go home," Grace said. "Or Mom'll be hollering for me to set the table."

She followed her brother and his girlfriend into the house. I got up to go in mine. The mail still hadn't come. I figured I might as well make myself a sandwich and start my essay.

The essay was a pain. After I wrote the title down, "How I Get Help When I Need It," then what? I could think of three sentences. Go talk to my mom. Go talk to the principal. Go talk to the reverend. There was no point in adding, Go talk to the teacher. Hillard was nice enough, but he'd be pretty useless.

72

I erased "reverend" and wrote in "friend." I might tell Pete something. Or maybe Grace, if she could keep her mouth shut. But I wasn't about to trot next door and ask to see the reverend.

The person I'd really like to talk to was my dad. I put down my pen and went out to check the mailbox. Aw right! There were two letters from him. One for me and one for Mom.

I dropped hers on the kitchen table beside my essay, got my jacket, and took my letter up to the tree house. The first thing that came out of the envelope was a twenty-dollar bill. Dad wrote that it was for Mom's Christmas present. He said he was sending Mom some money for my Christmas present. I wondered how much that would be.

Dad explained that he knew it wasn't even Thanksgiving yet, but he wanted to send the money before he lost it gambling. Then he added, "Heh! Heh!" Sometimes he gets too corny.

He said he knew Mom liked chocolate-covered cherries. Not the cheap kind you get in a white box in the drug store. But dark chocolate, the expensive kind you get at Frederick and Nelson's in the Everett Mall. I wondered how I was going to get to the mall without Mom. On the Metro, I guessed.

He ended his letter saying he'd been moved into a new room and he couldn't see the North Star. I didn't think they called them "rooms" in prison. I thought they called them cells. Maybe he didn't want to say cell in his letter to me.

The last thing he wrote was that even if he couldn't see the star, he thought about me every night. I folded

73

the letter and put it back in the envelope, wondering when he was going to get a parole. He hadn't said anything about that.

It was almost dark and the lights were on in Grace's house. Feeling lonesome, I looked down into the Elliotts' kitchen. The blinds were open and I could see the whole family.

Grace was setting the table, the redhead was grating carrots, and Mrs. Elliott had the oven open and was spooning fat over roasting chickens. Matt and the reverend were leaning back in chairs. Matt turned his head toward the counter and said something to the redhead. Everyone laughed. They all looked so happy down there.

Even when my dad was home, we never had a family like that. Dad's friends came over and sat around drinking beer. Rattler was there a lot and he'd send out for pizzas and we'd all pig out. Mom never cooked much.

I don't remember my dad ever getting up in the morning to go to a job like other kids' dads. When people asked him where he worked, he always said he was self-employed. If they got nosey and wanted to know what he did, he said he was a mechanic.

I thought that's what he was. I thought it was neat to have him work at home. When he didn't have a car in the garage, he would spend the afternoon playing basketball with me.

Dad had to make a lot of trips to meet people. Sometimes he'd take me along. We'd usually go up to the Park and Ride off Highway 9. When his customer would arrive, Dad'd hop out of our car, open the trunk, and lift out a car part. The man would look it over carefully, hand Dad some bills, and take off with the part.

I asked him a couple times where he got all the spare parts. He always said they came off the cars he repaired in our garage. I kept wondering how the cars could run with so many pieces gone.

Dad hauled the cars in and out when I was at school or after I'd gone to bed. Once in a while I'd watch him and Rattler work on one, but it got boring standing around the garage. One week, though, Mom sent me out there three days in a row. She was sewing curtains for her bedroom and didn't want to stop every time there was a phone call for Dad.

Each time I went to get him, the car they were working on looked barer. After Dad left for the phone, I told Rattler that it seemed like they were wrecking the car instead of fixing it. He said that was because it was a junker. When they got junkers, they just stripped them down and sold the pieces.

"Oh," I said, "Dad never explained that to me."

There were a few other things Dad hadn't explained. I found them out the day before my ninth birthday. I remember I was feeling great on the way home from school. I'd shot more baskets than any other kid in my PE class.

I was whistling as I rounded the corner by our old house. But what I saw then made my breath stop in my throat. Two police cars were parked in our yard. A third was parked in our driveway, blocking the entrance to the garage. As I slowly, fearfully drew nearer, the sound of cops on walkie-talkies grew louder.

That was the end of my good times. And the beginning of the bad times. I don't whistle anymore.

Grace doesn't know how lucky she is. She doesn't know how dumb she is sometimes, either. Life is simple when you're in the middle of your family eating roast chicken.

It was freezing cold up in the fir tree. I got down and went back into the house. I figured I might as well finish my essay. There was nothing else to do.

11

Five-Finger Discount

When I brought my essay in to Mrs. Nettle Monday morning, I told her it was pretty short. "That's all right," she said, "as long as you've made the point that there are other ways to solve problems besides fighting."

I nodded obediently.

Troller wasn't around at recess. I hoped he'd been kicked out of the school. He was there on Thursday, though. Maybe Mrs. Nettle just gave him a three-day suspension. Or maybe he'd been in bed for three days because of the beating I was sure he got from his old man. Anyway, he kept to the fourth-grade side of the playground.

After school I asked Grace what she thought my mom would like for Christmas. Even expensive chocolates couldn't cost twenty dollars. Grace suggested things like potholders and wooden spoons. Her mom might get off on a potholder, but a waitress wouldn't.

The week before Thanksgiving an ad in the newspaper gave me an idea for a present. A store in the mall was having a pre-Christmas sale. All shoes were marked down one third. Winter shoes and resort shoes, the ad said.

"Hey, Mom," I hollered. "If there's a shoe sale, what do they mean by 'resort shoes'?"

It was Sunday and she was in the bedroom getting fixed up to visit Dad. "That means they're unloading their leftover summer stock," she yelled back.

Perfect, I thought. There would be white shoes at the sale. Mom had to wear white shoes to go with her white uniform. And since the ad called them "resort shoes," they should be fancy. Fancy sandals were just what Mom needed. Flat ones, so her leg veins wouldn't pop out.

I was on my stomach reading the funnies when Mom leaned down to kiss me good-bye. "I won't be too late," she said. "We'll have dinner together."

I didn't care if she was late. I just wanted her to get out of the house. As soon as I heard her car start up, I was on my feet. Ten minutes later I was at the bus stop. Twenty-five minutes later, I was at the mall. It wasn't hard to find the shoe store, because there were big banners hanging over the windows announcing the sale.

A series of racks stood in the middle of the store. That's where all the women seemed to be huddling, so I joined them. At first, every shoe I turned over was size seven. I'd looked at Mom's shoes and they were five and a half. I went on to the second rack, but every shoe there was size eight.

Then I discovered the size signs at the edge of the racks. Okay, so I burrowed past three teenage girls and landed myself in front of the five-and-a-halfs.

Most of them were black or brown with needle heels and pointy toes.

There was a white moccasin with tassels that was kinda neat. But forty-nine dollars was crossed out on the sticker and thirty-two dollars and thirty-four cents was inked in. That much for just a moccasin?

I went down the rack a second time. There was nothing good except the moccasins. I wasn't even sure if Mom would like those. I wandered over to the shoes displayed on tables. There were some sandals in pink and blue and gold. No white, though.

I was about to take off when I spotted the sign on a shelf on the wall. Viper Snake and Calf. Viper snake? Scattered around the sign were pairs of tan sandals and white sandals. They had two diagonal bands crossing in front. The scaly band must be the snake-skin and the smooth one the calf.

I picked through the white sandals until I found one in size five and a half. Lucky! But the sticker said fifty-six seventy-six. Marked down from eighty-five. For two straps and a slab of leather? I put the sandal back on the shelf.

Still, they were too cool. I unzipped the top of my jacket while I checked out the store. A salesman was eyeing me. Whoa! How come?

On a couch near the shelves, a fat lady was trying on shoes. I edged over and sat down beside her, hoping the salesman would take me for her son. I acted really interested while she pulled on a pair of silver high heels. When she got up to to turn this way and that in front of a mirror, I stroked my chin thoughtfully.

The fat lady sat back down. She peered at her feet.

79

She frowned toward the counter. Her salesman must be up there. No time to waste. I took a quick glance around. Everybody busy.

I slipped off the couch, bellied up to the shelves, dropped the white sandals down the front of my jacket, and strolled toward the store entrance. My eyes looked straight ahead. My heart raced. My hand casually tapped the edge of the table that sat near the door.

I felt a man come beside me. My breath caught. He passed me, followed by a woman carrying a package.

I was out the door. I was halfway down the mall. I dropped down on a wooden bench that sat in the middle of the passageway. I heaved out a big sigh. Safe!

People trotted by me. The signs flickered on the stores. For a while I barely saw anything. Then gradually I steadied myself and looked around.

The Baskin-Robbins sign urged me to get off the bench. I could feel the chocolate fudge ice cream slip over my tongue. But how was I going to keep a grip on the shoes, pay the clerk, and take the cone?

A trash bin stood in front of PayLess. That might do it. Holding my arm tight against my jacket, I got up, took the lid off the bin, and rummaged through the burrito wrappers and Pepsi-Cola cups to find a sack big enough for the shoes. A Hallmark sack was too crumpled. The plastic B. Dalton one was like new. Aw right!

I took a quick look around, flapped the sack open, stuck it under the front of my jacket, and lifted my arm. The sandals fell neatly into the bag.

I beat Mom back home by half an hour. That gave me plenty of time to hide the sandals and box of cherry chocolates behind my boots in the closet. I put the *faux* tortoiseshell barrette on the table beside my bed.

That's what the saleslady had called the yellow-brown barrette: *faux* tortoiseshell. I'd spied it on a counter in Frederick and Nelson's after I bought the chocolates. I'd asked the saleslady what the *faux* part meant. She said it meant imitation. She said it was against the law to have a real tortoiseshell. Real or not, the barrette was cooler than the stupid ribbons Grace put in her hair.

Luckily, Mom helped me wrap it after she got home, because Grace came over Tuesday. It was raining and she came right in the house to play checkers with me. I guess she figured she couldn't get yelled at since her mom was at a meeting.

Grace beat me once and then I beat her twice. "Change seats with me," she said. "You must have the lucky one."

After she settled in my place, she asked, "Did you hear all the screaming at our house last night?"

"No, I didn't hear anything."

"Well." Grace paused to help me set up a new game. "Mom got up in the night to go to the bathroom and found out that Matt wasn't home. She got all excited and made Dad get up. He was trying to talk her out of calling the police when I came in the living room.

"And then Matt walked in the door and she started

81

yelling that it was three o'clock and what was he doing until three o'clock in the morning. Dad tried to calm her down, but she wanted to know if that redhead was out too. When Matt said yes, Mom wanted to know what kind of a girl could stay out until three on a school night. Then Matt got mad and said he was leaving."

Grace had been so busy talking that I was able to jump two of her pieces. "Did he leave?"

She frowned at the board. "No." While concentrating on her next move, she seemed to forget her story.

"What did your folks do about Matt?" I prompted her.

"Oh, Dad told me and Mom to go on to bed. He said he'd take care of Matt." Grace pushed a black checker forward and sat back to wait for me.

I moved a red one. "Did your dad give Matt a bad time?"

"Probably not," Grace said. "Nothing ever happens to him. Except Mom screams a lot."

I thought to myself that I'd lucked out more with my mom than Grace had with hers. The game ended with me winning. I got up to get us some Pepsis.

We drank the Pepsis and I teased Grace about beating her again. I must have felt good, like I really had a friend, because I burst out, "Wanna see what I got my mom for Christmas?"

"Sure," she said.

I hauled out the sandals.

Grace turned them over in her hands. "Gol, these are neat. Snakeskin. Gol, they cost enough."

"Naw," I said. "I got them at a five-finger discount."

"A what?" she said.

"A five-finger discount." I picked at the air with my fingers. "Five fingers, dummy."

Big mistake. Her eyes grew wide. She shoved the sandals back at me as if the viper were alive. "Don't ever give me a Christmas present," she told me. "I don't want any stolen goods." And she marched out of my house.

12

A Mean Face

Grace didn't talk to me much after she found out I swiped the sandals. When she did talk to me, she sounded like we were at a tea party. "Isn't it just freezing today?" or "I hope Mr. Hillard lets us decorate a tree."

I wanted to ask her if she'd blabbed about the sandals to her dad. But she acted like it'd never happened. So I acted like it never happened too.

She thawed out a little after Hillard assigned the parts for our Christmas play. She got Mrs. Cratchett and I got Bob Cratchett. I get mostly C's in school, but I'm good when it comes to plays.

I had my lines learned in two days. So did Pete, who was Scrooge. He and I tossed a ball around the gym, where we were practicing while Grace and the other kids stumbled through their scripts.

We put on the play the night before winter vacation. Mom said I was the best one in the cast. Even Mrs. Nettle complimented me. On the way home, Mom and I stopped for root beer floats. We were both feeling high. Partly because of the play and partly because Dad had written that he was coming home in January.

"I hope we never have another Christmas without your father," Mom said.

"I hope so too," I told her, and slurped the last of my root beer up through the straw.

Christmas morning was as good as it could be without my dad. Mom got all swimmy-eyed over the sandals. She put them on and paraded around the house. "They're so comfortable! They're a perfect fit. How did you do it?" She swished her hips while she held her hand in the air as if she were carrying a tray full of dishes. "I'm going to look so-o class-y."

I didn't cry over my presents, but I sure liked them. I got the sleeping bag I wanted so I could sleep up in my tree house sometimes. I also got a Swatch, which I hadn't asked for but liked even more than the sleeping bag.

I hugged Mom after I ripped open the package and found the red watch with its see-through insides. "This is cool," I told her. "How'd you know about Swatch watches?"

"Oh, I get around," she said.

Pete had a Swatch. So did Mari. I figured that with it and my Generra jacket nobody would be able to tell me from a regular kid.

When she'd gathered up all the wrappings and stuffed them in the garbage, Mom asked me, "Are you going to give Grace her present?"

"I might as well," I said. There was no way I could explain to Mom why I didn't want to give Grace a present anymore.

I felt stupid ringing the Elliotts' doorbell while holding the fancy package in my hand. Grace answered, took one look at the present, backed up a bit, and said, "Hi. Merry Christmas. Um, come on in."

"No thanks, PK. I just wanted to give you this." I shoved the present at her. "It's paid for."

Grace took the present from me. Her cheeks had turned bright pink. "Please come in a minute. I've got something for you."

I didn't believe that. "Naw, I gotta go."

"Just wait a sec." She dashed toward the kitchen and came back carrying a paper plate of cookies. They were wrapped in plastic with a green bow stuck on top. "Here, Merry Christmas."

I thanked her, turned, and walked down the steps with the cookies. Grace's cheeks had stayed pink. I didn't know then why *she* should be embarrassed, but I found out later that morning.

Mom had a stack of pancakes waiting when I got back. After we'd finished them off and Mom was sipping her coffee, she said, "You know what I'd like to do today?"

"No, what?"

"I'd like to go to the church down the street."

That was about the last thing I wanted to do. "When?" I asked. "This afternoon?"

"No, this morning. There's a service at ten o'clock. If we hurry, we can make it."

I checked my Swatch. Unfortunately, she was right.

I put on a clean shirt. Mom dressed up in a red suit and black high heels. I guess she couldn't wear white sandals in December.

The choir was singing "Joy to the World" when we came in the church door. They switched to "O Little Town of Bethlehem" as we slipped into an empty place in one of the middle pews. Before I slouched down, I spotted Grace in one of the front pews. I couldn't see if she had the barrette in her hair, but there was no dumb ribbon stuck on her head.

The choir finished up with a song about sweet little baby Jesus. While the singers closed their hymn books, Reverend Elliott moved to the pulpit. "In our rejoicing in the birth of our savior . . ." he began, his bass voice rumbling out of his big chest.

I checked my Swatch. This shouldn't take more than an hour.

Reverend Elliott went on about how Christmas isn't only a time for the symbolic giving of presents, but also a time to look into ourselves to see how closely we pattern our lives on Jesus. "For as surely as we do unto others, we do unto ourselves," he thundered. "Do you believe your evil behavior doesn't stick to you? Do you think it doesn't show?"

In a softer voice he told of taking his son for a walk when his son was four. During the walk, a man nodded a greeting to them. When the man had passed, his son said, "That man has a mean face."

"My son was right! That man also had a mean heart." Reverend Elliott had turned up the volume again. "If you looked into Bob Cratchett's face, could you tell he was a good man? If you looked into Scrooge's face, could you tell he was a selfish man?"

I pictured my dad's face. I saw the gap-toothed smile that everyone trusted. The one that is just like mine. I poked my tongue between my teeth while Reverend Elliott told a story about chickens.

He said it was Baba Ram Dass's story, whoever that is. He said there was a man who had three sons. He gave each of his sons a chicken. He told them to go out where they couldn't be seen and kill the chickens.

The first and second sons came back with dead chickens, but the third son came back with a live chicken. When the father asked the third son why he hadn't killed his chicken, the son said, "Everywhere I go, the chicken sees."

Anyway, I thought, shoes aren't a chicken.

Reverend Elliott bellowed, "Do you think there's a place where you can't be seen?

"When a man steals . . ." Reverend Elliott paused, and his words hit through to my bones, "he steals from himself. As ye sow, so shall ye reap!

"Let us pray."

While everyone else was praying, I was thinking of Grace's pink cheeks. She had plenty of reason to be embarrassed. She'd squealed on me to her old man. And he must have spotted me in the pew. He didn't say anything about killing or swearing. Just stealing.

Reverend Elliott was at the door to greet the people leaving the church. I tried to push Mom by him, but she had to stop. While she shook his hand and told him what an inspiring sermon he'd preached, I went on down the steps.

When Mom caught up with me, she was quiet until we were almost to our house. Then she said, "Your dad better be careful of his face."

89

I hated it when she warned me about my dad. What could I do about it? It just made me feel bad.

In bed that night, though, I wondered if he would look different when he came home.

Grace showed up in my backyard a couple days after Christmas. I was there alone shooting baskets. She stood around and watched me a few minutes before she asked me to come over to her house. She had a new chess set and wanted to know if I'd like to learn the game.

"I already know how to play chess," I told her.

"Then you could teach me."

I aimed at the hoop, made the shot, and caught the ball on the first bounce. "Are you sure your mother wants a rip-off in her house?"

"My mother doesn't know anything about you," Grace said quietly.

I tried for another basket and missed. "But your dad knows everything, doesn't he, PK?"

"Well, he's different. He doesn't mind."

"He doesn't mind, huh? What exactly did he say after you blabbed about the sandals?"

"He said . . ." She stared at the ball I was bouncing in front of her, took in a big breath, and went on. "He said I could be a good example for you."

I laughed in her face. "Get real, PK!"

She pinked up again. I turned and concentrated on shooting baskets, totally ignoring her. After a while I thought I felt her leaving. I held the ball. Looked around. She was gone.

I sat down on the ground, holding the ball to my stomach. I'd been lonesome before, but not this much.

13

Lost and Found

On the Thursday after Christmas I went grocery shopping with Mom. She thought she'd bought everything at Safeway, but on the way home she clapped her hand to her forehead. "Darn, I forgot coffee!"

We were up by Mill Creek, because she'd dropped into her chiropractor's to pay the bill. A 7 Eleven was nearby. Mom pulled in the parking lot. I followed her inside the store, hoping for a candy bar.

She went for the coffee and I went for a bar. I was at the counter deciding between a Butterfinger and a Snickers, when I felt somebody watching me. I turned my head. There by the magazine rack was Troller with a couple of older kids.

One of the guys flipped a thumb toward my jacket. Troller nodded. He was watching me with his lids halfway down over his eyes. That's his idea of a wiseguy, I guess.

I picked up a Snickers and handed it to Mom so she could pay for it. Then, ignoring Troller, I followed her out of the store. Before she started up the car, she said, "Edward and his friends look like little hoods."

"They are," I said.

On the rest of the way home, I munched on my candy and thought about Troller and his friends. They all had old, pinched faces. Grace and her friends had young, plump faces.

I helped Mom carry in the groceries and then I headed straight for the bathroom. I leaned over the sink to peer at myself in the mirror. My face looked okay to me. But just in case, I decided to drink an extra glass of milk every morning.

The winter vacation was over two days after New Year's Eve. Much to my relief. I don't think school's so neat, but watching TV and shooting basketballs by myself was getting to be much. I even said hi to Grace when she came out of her house to walk to the bus.

As soon as she'd caught up with me, she turned her head so I could see the tortoiseshell barrette. It reminded me of her squealing about the sandals to her dad. I didn't say it looked good in her hair.

The quieter I got, the more Grace chattered. It was like the power between us had shifted. First, I'd thought we were friends and told her too much. Then I wasn't good enough for her. Then she pulled that stuff about being an example for me, which made me puke. Now she was all over me.

"Oh, gol, you've got a Swatch watch. They're so cool. I wish I had one. Mari and Nicky and Pete have them, you know. Except I like yours best. I like the see-throughs, don't you."

94

I climbed on the bus ahead of her without answering. Let her sweat awhile.

Mr. Hillard started off our class with "Get out your brainstorming chart and a piece of scratch paper. I'll give you one minute."

I rummaged in my desk for some old paper. I still hadn't found anything when Hillard warned, "Four more seconds."

I ripped a clean sheet from my notebook and sat up straight.

Hillard rubbed his hands together and gave us a smile. He must have gotten rested over vacation. "First, we'll have a practice session to warm up your brains. We'll use words that have to do with holidays."

"Any holidays?" Susan asked.

"Any holidays." Hillard looked at the clock. "All right, now. Start."

I wrote as fast as I could. Reindeers, presents, candy canes, party, pumpkins, candles, trees . . . I crossed out trees and wrote Christmas trees. I shouldn't have taken the time. Now I couldn't think of another holiday word. Easter? Easter? Bunnies, eggs, nests . . .

"Stop! Put down your pencils." Hillard looked around the room to be sure we all obeyed. "How many got twenty-five words?"

Two kids raised their hands.

"How many got twenty words?"

More kids raised their hands.

"Very good," Hillard said. "Now for the real one. Things that fly. Starting . . . Now!"

This time I was going to keep going. Birds, bees, airplane, sparrow, leaves, seeds, butterfly, 747, hydroplane . . . Hmm, I didn't know about hydroplane. Keep going, stupid. Ummm, ummm. Fleas. No, they hopped. Mosquito, fly, helicopter—

"Stop! Count your words. Record the number."

I only got twelve. Same as the last time we did it.

"Clear your desks," Hillard demanded. "And then I want you to think about how the things you wrote down stay up in the air."

Pete raised his hand. "I wrote cannonball."

"How does it stay up in the air?" Hillard asked.

"Power," Pete said.

"I put down airplane . . ." Susan's voice dribbled away. I knew she didn't know how they stayed in the air.

"It's a four-letter word," Hillard told her.

"Lift!" Mari burst out.

Hillard nodded, took a sheet of paper from the table beside him, and let it float down to the floor. He crumpled another piece of paper and let that drop to the floor. He stared at us with eyebrows raised.

Grace waved her hand. "If a paper's flat, it drops slower."

Pete's hand shot up. "There's more surface area on a flat piece of paper."

Pete's smart.

Hillard drew a parachute on the board and we were off on a discussion of how weight, shape, and material affect flight. It was pretty interesting. In fact, I was surprised when it was time for recess.

I was too happy playing one-on-one with Pete to even look for Troller. After recess our class went to the library. I still had on my jacket. It got warm while I was

96

reading, so I took it off and put it on the back of my chair.

I didn't think about my jacket again until we were lining up to go out after lunch. When I remembered where it was, I hurried over to Kathy and got a library pass. "Hey?" Pete objected.

"Just have to get my jacket," I told him, and hurried down the hall.

My jacket wasn't on the chairs anywhere. I asked Mr. Folsom if he'd seen it. He shook his head thoughtfully. "No, no one's turned anything in. But I've been busy at the counter. Classes have been in here all morning. Why don't you try the lost and found in the office?"

I went for the office. The secretary was busy at the copy machine. I stood on one foot and then the other foot until he finished. "Where's the lost and found?" I asked him when he came to the counter.

"Right there." He pointed to a cardboard box that was sitting by the door.

I pawed through it. Nothing but old sweaters, baseball caps, and mittens. I heaved a sigh as I dropped a blue cap back on the pile.

The secretary was watching me. "Can't find what you lost?"

"No, it's a gray jacket. I left it in the library. You haven't seen it?"

He shook his head and turned to a girl who'd just come in carrying a note. The girl handed the secretary the note, then turned to me. "I saw a fourth-grade kid wearing a jacket outside that was way too big for him."

"Edward Troller?"

97

"I don't know his name, but he's got dark hair and is kinda pointy-faced."

"That's Troller, the little rip-off!"

Before I could get to the door, Mrs. Nettle collared me. I hadn't even seen her come out of her office. "Just a minute, Jerry! I'll take care of this. You go sit in my office."

"I haven't done anything bad."

"And you're not going to. You wait for me in my office." She took off and I went in and sat on one of her wooden chairs.

I was staring out her window at the kids coming in from recess when Mrs. Nettle came back holding Troller by his arm. He was dragging my jacket along with two fingers. His face had that greenish color again.

"Is this your jacket?" Mrs. Nettle asked me.

"Yes, it is," I said.

"Give it to Jerry," she told Troller.

He silently handed over the jacket. As I took it I saw why he'd been carrying it by his fingers. There was gum stuck on the shoulder, banana peel smeared on the back, and splotches of red ink all down the side. I looked up at Mrs. Nettle. "He trashed it!" I couldn't believe it. "He trashed it!" I said again.

"Yes, he tried to hide it in the garbage. Somebody must have thrown a broken colored marker in the can. You might be able to clean the jacket if the ink isn't permanent. Where did you you get it?"

"At the Brethren House."

"Oh, that's lucky. Then it didn't cost you anything."

"Lucky?" Did she think I could get a free Generra

98

jacket any day? "Lucky?" I know I stared at her as if she were nuts. Then I turned to Troller. Every muscle in my body wanted to jump him.

Troller shrank behind Mrs. Nettle. She gave his arm a shake. "Go sit down," she told him.

He made a wide circle around me. She went to her desk and poked the numbers on her phone. "Mr. Troller, please," she said.

Edward Troller turned even greener.

"Mr. Troller," Mrs. Nettle said into the phone, "this is Wilma Nettle."

Edward shriveled in his chair. Mrs. Nettle caught my eye and nodded her head toward the door, meaning I should leave.

I closed the door slowly behind me, not looking back at Troller. He knew he was going to get beaten, all right. Only it wasn't going to be by me. Revenge for what he did to my jacket was sweet, but I feel a little sick thinking how big his fat, old man was.

"Here," the secretary said, "you'll need an admit slip to get into your class."

"Oh, ya, thanks." I took the pass and headed for the boys' can.

A lump of the pink bubble gum came up when I pulled at it with a paper towel. But when I tried to scrub off the rest, pieces of the towel stuck in the cloth. I gave up and tried to soak out the red ink. Not a chance. I hauled the soppy, wet jacket back to Hillard's class.

"Cripes, that thing stinks like rotten bananas," Pete said.

14

Something in Me

Where were you at noon?" Grace asked on our way home from school.

"Getting my jacket back from Troller," I told her. "He took it out of the library and dumped it in a garbage can."

"I was wondering why you were carrying it." She pulled at a bare branch hanging over the sidewalk. "Anyway, now you know how it feels to have someone steal from you."

"Drop dead, PK," I said, and hurried on ahead of her.

She ran to catch up with me. I kept going. She walked as fast as I did. "I'm sorry, Jerry. I don't know what's the matter with me. Sometimes I sound just like my mom."

"Sometimes you sound like an idiot," I said.

"I know. Come on. We're friends, aren't we?"

I didn't know about that.

"Come on. Please," she begged. "I'll even let you beat me at chess."

"You don't have to let me. I'll beat you anyway."

101

"I know. Come, on. Come on over to my house and play me a game."

I slowed down. She was the only one in the neighborhood. And she wasn't so bad when she didn't act like a mother. "I gotta do some stuff first. I'll be over in a little while."

That made Grace smile. She patted the barrette on the back of her head. "I sure like this better than my ribbons."

"Those ribbons made you look like a nerd."

Her smile wobbled, but she kept it on her face. I gave her a good-bye jerk of my head and crossed over to my yard.

After I made myself a sandwich, I tipped back in a kitchen chair to eat and think. I didn't have to know how it felt to be ripped off. Getting ripped off again is what I didn't want. I'm not especially religious. But that "as ye sow so shall ye reap" had me worried. I decided I'd better not leave my sleeping bag in the tree house anymore. Somebody might climb up there and get it.

And I wished I hadn't told Grace I'd come over. Her dad should be at his church in the afternoon. But how could I be sure? It would be embarrassing to meet him again face-to-face. I hated having him know I was a thief. I wished I could get rid of the stupid sandals.

I left half the sandwich on the kitchen table and got up to empty the sink. When it was clean, I filled it with soapy water and dipped the back of my jacket in. The soap took out the banana stains, but not the gum. That came off with an SOS pad. Nothing removed the ink.

I hung the jacket up in my bedroom and stood

staring at the red blots. Maybe I could camouflage them by drawing flames up the side. But maybe that would make a worse mess. Maybe I could try just a small flame to see how it worked.

Back in the kitchen, I ate a couple bites of the sandwich. It was too dry. I threw the crust of bread in the garbage and went on over to Grace's.

Mrs. Elliott had brownies and apple juice waiting for us. The brownies had nuts and raisins in them and tasted great. I told Mrs. Elliott so. That seemed to please her, only I couldn't really tell if she liked me or not. I wished I hadn't spit on her party dress.

Reverend Elliott came in while Grace and I were in the middle of our second game. I didn't have the guts to say hello. I just kept my burning face bent over the chessboard.

Grace was taking forever to make her move. She had her finger on her bishop and a frown on her face. Finally, she pulled the bishop back, moved a pawn forward, and kept her finger on that.

Reverend Elliott was standing by the coffee table watching us. When Grace pulled her pawn back, I dared to take a quick glance at him. He gave me a sympathetic smile and a pat on the shoulder before he left the room. He had such a warm feel about him that I couldn't help but like him.

We were starting our third game when Mrs. Elliott came in and said it was time for Grace to set the dinner table. I popped to my feet. "I didn't realize it was so late," I told her.

"That's all right. That's all right." She put a hand

103

out to calm me down. "We eat early so Grace's father can get back to his office to counsel."

"Oh. Right. Thanks for the brownies. I'll see ya, Grace." I nodded at them both and got out of there.

On the way home, I thought the reverend must spend a lot of time counseling. His office was probably in his church. I wondered who came to see him.

Mom got up the next morning to make my breakfast. This was a change. "What are you doing up at seven-thirty?" I asked her.

"I'm taking an extra day off this week." Smiles were curling all over her face.

"What's going on?" Anytime she got up before nine in the morning something had to be happening.

"You'll find out," she said. "Do you want some pancakes?"

"Sure." I watched her suspiciously while she bent to get the pancake mix out of bottom cupboard. Something had to be . . . "It's Dad! Dad's coming home today!"

She put the sack on the counter and opened the refrigerator for eggs and milk. I closed it after her. "Come on, Dad's out on parole, isn't he?"

"You'll find out." She turned away from me to get a bowl out of the top cupboard.

I pulled a chair away from the kitchen table, switched it around, and sat down, leaning my chin on the back of it. "I'm not going to school today."

"Yes, you are." She concentrated on beating the eggs and milk.

"No, I'm not."

"Set the table," she said.

I thought a minute. Should I give in and set the table or not? I decided to set it. The table really wasn't the point. We were silent while I got out the knives and forks and she heated up the frying pan.

When the pancakes were done, she put a stack on a warm plate and handed it to me. I smeared the pancakes with butter and syrup and began wolfing them down. She brought her plate and cup to the table and sat beside me.

She ate quietly for a few minutes and then poked me in the ribs. "Go on to school today," she said softly. "It's been a long time, and I need to be alone with him for a while."

I looked into her face. My mom really has a sweet face. Especially in the morning when she isn't wearing any makeup. The gray eyes that looked into mine were glowing with excitement.

I poked her back. "Okay, but I don't know how I'll stand school today."

"You can stand it for me," she said.

I guessed so. But it wasn't easy. On a regular day school's boring enough. And on this day I thought it would go on forever.

We had library fifth period. Library usually goes by fast. Only this time Mr. Folsom had prepared a card catalog quiz. About five of us didn't have our pencils. He handed out four of his spare ones and then told me to run back to the room for mine.

While I was sharpening my pencil by Mr. Hillard's desk, I noticed his top drawer was open a little bit. My

105

hand reached down and pulled it out farther. There under his grade book were a pair of scissors and a box of colored markers.

Nobody was around. I figured Hillard was in the faculty room drinking coffee. My hand moved the grade book off the box. Here was my chance to fix the jacket. I could slip a red marker out easy. No problem.

My hand didn't pick up the box, though. Something in me didn't want to. Something in me didn't want to steal anymore.

"What are you doing in the room, Jerry?"

I looked up to see Mr. Hillard watching me from the door. "Folsom's having a test so he sent me to the room for my pencil. It needed sharpening," I explained while I silently eased the drawer shut with my hip.

"It's *Mister* Folsom, and you'd better get back to the library."

I nodded and hurried into the hall thinking, Whoa, lucky I didn't have those markers in my paws! Then Mr. Hillard and Mrs. Nettle and my mom would all know I was a thief.

Sixth period we had another test. It was on adverbs. Three long dittos of them. I filled in about three blanks, checked out my Swatch, then filled in three more.

After Mr. Hillard collected our papers, he settled down in front of the room to read to us. I checked my Swatch two more times. The hands were dragging toward three.

Pete fumbled in his desk for a pencil. Hillard didn't mind if we drew while he was reading. "Hey," I whispered to Pete. "Have you got any red and yellow pens?"

"Sure." He pulled them out and gave them to me.

I took my jacket off the back of my chair and spread it on our table. Pete watched while I tried to make the blots into flames. His red marker was too light. "Here," he whispered, "try blue."

I made the bottom of the flames blue, or sort of a muddy blue, and the tops red and yellow. The flames looked a little real. Not great. But better than just ink stains.

Hillard closed his book. "Kathy, will you get the class ready for dismissal."

At last!

15

Dad's Home

What's the matter with you?" Grace asked as she jumped off the bus after me. "What's the big rush?"

"My dad's home," I said.

"Your dad's home! Gol, I'd like to see him. What does he look like?"

"Me," I said, and zipped on ahead, down the street, across her yard and over the bushes. What would he look like? Would he look like a convict? Would he be changed?

The front door flew open just as I hit the bottom step. When I reached the edge of the porch, he snatched me up and whirled me around in a big bear hug.

"My boy! My boy! Let me see you!" He let go of my waist, pushed me back from him by my shoulders, and peered into my face. There were tears in his eyes. "You're bigger," he said. "Oh, God, you've grown. I've missed so much!"

"You haven't grown," I said.

He laughed and hugged me again. "No, I'm just the same."

And he was, too. There wasn't anything bad in his face. He had that big, pumpkin smile just as he always had. Maybe Reverend Elliott didn't know what he was talking about.

"Let's go around back. I've got a surprise for you." He kept his arm around my shoulders as he led me into the backyard. "Well, how do you like it?"

At first I didn't know what he meant. And then I spied it, leaning against the side of the garage. "Oh. Oh, a ten-speed!" I walked up to it slowly, reached out my hand, and stroked the gleaming blue bars. "I never thought I'd ever have one of these."

"Pretty neat, huh?" Dad said. "It's a Peugeot. Your mom and I picked it out this afternoon."

That was a relief! If my mom helped pick it out, it wasn't a hot bike. Nobody could come and take it away. "Jeez, it must've cost a lot of money," I said.

"Ya, well, I saved some of my pay. While I was in . . . a . . . that place, I planned just what I was going to get you when I got out. See, these two levers control the gears. This one controls the rear sprockets, and this one controls the two front sprockets. You're not supposed to change gears unless you're pedaling."

"I know," I told him. "When we were in our old house, Jimmy used to let me ride his ten-speed sometimes."

Dad wasn't listening. He was bending down beside the bike. "And see, I had them put on these toe clips so your feet won't come off the pedals when you're riding on hills."

I didn't know about toe clips. Kids don't use those.

Just old people have toe clips. I didn't say anything about that, though.

"And look." Dad patted the curled handlebars. "There are four brake handles—"

"I know. Jimmy's had—"

"See," Dad went on, "there are two on top and two underneath."

"It's sure cool," I said, curving my fingers around the center bar.

"Ya, it is." Dad stood back, admiring the bike. "Why don't you try it out?"

"Okay." I walked the bike out to the sidewalk, over the curb, and onto the street. I hopped up on the seat, stuck my toes in the clips, and took off. I was down at the end of the block in a flash. The thing went like the wind.

"One hand!" I waved at Dad as I zipped by him.

"No hands," I yelled as I came down the block again. Then I grabbed the handlebars quick. I'd almost tipped over. It'd been a long time since I rode a bike.

I stopped in front of Dad, who was standing at the curb. "You want to try it?"

"Sure," he said. I got off. He got on.

I watched him go up and down the block. Every once in a while he lifted his hands off the bars. Each time he did the bike wobbled. He couldn't ride as well as I could.

I was getting anxious for him to quit. I wanted to ride again. When he finally did slow up, he made the mistake of shifting gears after he'd stopped pedaling. This made the chain fall off.

111

He hopped off the bike and wheeled it up on the grass. "No big deal," he said. "I can fix it."

I stood impatiently watching him get his hands all greasy trying to put the chain back on. "Here, let me help," I said.

We'd just gotten the chain fixed when Mom came out the front door. "Come on in, you two kids," she hollered. "Dinner's ready."

"Aw, I wanted to have another ride," I told Dad.

"You can, after dinner. Let's go in. She's probably knocked herself out making something special."

She had. It was chicken fried steaks, baked potatoes with sour cream, and a big fruit salad. "Sure better than I've been getting," Dad said.

"Better than I've been getting too," I said.

Mom and Dad laughed. They were looking so happy. And I was so happy too.

Dad and I took turns riding the bike after dinner. When the dishes were done, Mom came out. Dad had her sit on the seat. He climbed on in front of her and rode her down the block. At first she held on tight. But when she stopped being scared, she let go of his waist and waved her hands in the wind like a young girl.

It got dark too soon. Dad walked across our lawn holding Mom's hand. I rode the bike behind them, bumped it up the steps, and wheeled it in the door.

"Wait just a minute!" Mom'd stopped in front of me. "That docsn't belong in the house."

"I'm keeping it in my room," I explained. "It might get ripped off if I leave it outside."

"Well, leave it on the porch," she said.

"Oh, let him bring it in," Dad told her. "Somebody might steal it."

"Not on the porch," she objected.

"You'd be surprised," he said.

"Well, you know more about that than I do." Her sharp tone cut through the air.

The happiness drained from Dad's face. "Things are going to be different," he said.

She reached one hand to his cheek. She had her other hand over her mouth as if to keep more bad words from coming out. "I'm sorry, Jerry." She turned her head to me. "Go ahead and put the bike in your room."

I rolled it past them and into my bedroom and parked it in front of my closet. Right where I could see it if I woke up in the night.

16

Close Call

After school the next day Grace came over to see my ten-speed. I let her take a short ride. What I really wanted to do was take off by myself. Pete had told me his address and I wanted to see if I could at least find his neighborhood. Grace kept hanging and hanging on me, though.

I had my leg over the bike bar and was trying to be polite while I waited for her to leave. She was standing beside me chewing on her thumbnail.

"Matt's been working on Mom to get him a new transmission. He's been telling her that his car's going to break down in the middle of the road if he doesn't get it fixed."

"His car sure makes a racket." My leg was getting tired so I took it off the bar.

"Ya, and every time Mom complains about that, Matt explains about transmissions." Grace wiped her thumb across her T-shirt. "I think I'll tell her a bunch of times that the car sounds like it's falling apart. That'll make her get it fixed. Then she'll have to buy me a bike."

115

"Does a preacher make a lot of money?"

"My dad doesn't, but we've got a rich grandma and Mom can get money from her if she needs it."

"Lucky you," I said, rolling my bike back and forth on the parking strip.

"I suppose you want to go see Pete," she said.

"Ya, well, I'd like to see where his house is anyway."

"I better go, then." Grace turned and walked all by herself to her front door.

I felt a little guilty leaving her alone, knowing how that hurt. But as soon as I was flying down the street, I forgot about her.

Pete's neighborhood was on the top of three long hills. By the time I'd pumped up there, I was too beat to look for his house. I decided to wait for Saturday morning. It was a blast zooming back down the hills.

Dad pulled up in our car just as I got home. "Any luck with a job?" I asked him.

He leaned out the car window. "Naw, there was nothing. I think I need some new clothes. Or at least some better shoes. What say we pick up hamburgers and shop the mall?"

"Wait a sec until I put my bike away." I stashed it in my bedroom, took a leak, and joined Dad in the car.

I felt big and light driving with him. It'd been a long time. Almost two years. We were buddies again. He smoked cigarettes and I laughed at his jokes until we reached the mall.

The first thing we hit was a shoe store. Not the same one where I'd gotten Mom's sandals. But just as expensive. "Let's try Penney's," Dad said. "These prices are out of line."

116

The men's shoe department at Penney's had all kinds of stuff. Running shoes, loafers, saddles, boots. I called Dad over to see a pair of brown suede moccasins. "These would look cool with your suede jacket," I told him.

He turned one of the moccasins around in his hand, scrunched up his face, then shook his head. "No, I think I like the lizard loafers better."

"Lizard!" I said, following him over to another table. "Lizard will cost mass bucks."

He grinned his pumpkin-face grin. "Well . . ."

That was when fear coiled up in my stomach.

"May I help you, gentlemen?" a skinny, mustached salesman asked.

"Yes," Dad said, "I'd like to see these in size ten."

"Certainly. Would you like to take a seat over here? I'll be right back."

As I watched the salesman go into the stockroom, I blew air out of my mouth. I knew what was coming and it scared me more than any bad thing I'd ever done. At first I tried to make myself stay cool. Then the fear grew so big, I burst out, "What if you get . . ."

"Here you are, sir." The salesman sat down in front of Dad, took off his right shoe, and put on a loafer. "How's it feel?"

Dad wiggled his foot. "Feels pretty good."

The salesman took the other shoe out of the box. "Let's try them both on."

Dad stood up and bounced on his feet a couple times before he tilted his head thoughtfully at the loafers. "Do you have these in black?"

"Yes, we do."

117

As soon as the salesman had disappeared into the stockroom, Dad muttered, "Follow me."

He got up, casually strolled to a mirror, turned this way and that, moved to another mirror, and looked himself over. I fingered some saddles on a table, trying to watch the stockroom door at the same time. Dad edged across the middle aisle of the store and I followed. He moved over to a display of shirts near the entrance and pretended to read the advertisement.

Just as Dad whispered to me, "Okay, let's go," the salesman appeared. Out of the corner of my eye I saw him stare at our empty seats before he motioned to a man at the counter.

Dad hissed behind me. "Come on! Let's go!"

"Wait! Wait!" The salesman and the counterman were heading toward us. I dropped to the floor beside Dad and pinched the toes of his shoes. I could feel the men closing in. Beads of sweat covered my face as I said loudly, "They don't seem tight to me. Where do they hurt?"

Dad must have spotted the men, because he leaned down and pointed. "Right there by my little toe."

"Have you decided on these shoes?" The deep voice came from right above us.

We stood up to look into the cold eyes of the counterman. He must be the manager, I thought.

"Why, no." Dad answered the man, like he was real surprised. "The shoes seemed fine at first, but after I walked in them a bit, they began to hurt my toes." He gave the man his big gap-toothed smile.

The man smiled politely back, "We'd rather you'd stay on the carpet."

"Oh." Dad looked around like he hadn't even known he was at the tiled entrance. "I'm sorry. We'll get back on your rug."

That was supposed to make the man feel foolish, I knew. But the man didn't look like he was buying any of it. The sweat was running onto my neck by this time.

Dad stared at the man a second, shrugged, and walked across the aisle to the shoe department. I followed him to his old shoes, which he put on after he took off the loafers.

The salesman leaned down to put the loafers in the box. "Would you like to try a size ten and half?"

I wanted to burst out at Dad, jeez, no! Let's get out of here! I could hardly stand it while he pretended to decide whether he wanted to try on another size or not.

"Umm, not today. We've got quite a bit more shopping to do. Thanks, anyway."

I expected one of the men to grab us on our way back to the store entrance. The skin prickled on my shoulders waiting for their grasping fingers. None came.

Dad walked right out the door and down the mall. When we got to the benches I'd sat on before, I collapsed. Dad sat down beside me. For a minute I couldn't look at him. I was so upset over what he'd done.

"You don't have to sweat," he said. "Those jerks didn't know enough to wait until we were outside. They can't do anything while I'm still inside the mall."

"They could have waited," I said, "and caught us."

119

"Oh, ya." He seemed to wilt a little. "I guess that wasn't too smart of me."

"You could have been sent back up." I wanted to add, What about me? What about Mom and me? You told her things were going to be different. But he was looking down at his hands which were clasped between his legs. I didn't know what he was thinking and I didn't want to be mean to him.

He sighed. "I guess I'd better get some shoe polish and clean these old things up."

"You shouldn't have spent so much money on my bike," I said.

"No, I wanted you to have it. You got cheated on your old man. You should at least have a bike. Every boy should have one."

"I didn't get cheated on my old man. I think you're neat." I was having trouble keeping from crying.

He patted my shoulder. "Ah, it's just because you've never had another dad that you think I'm neat. Come on, let's stop in the drugstore for some shoe polish and then take off for home."

I trotted behind him into PayLess. I wanted to explain that I'd seen plenty of other dads. Troller's for instance. My dad had never hit me once. Even when I was a little kid.

I wanted to tell him again that he was a good father. I wanted to pretend that I wasn't ashamed of what he'd done. Or what I'd done. But he kept talking about other things and didn't give me a chance to explain any more about dads.

When we got home, we watched TV until Mom arrived. She came in carrying a six-pack of beer, which made Dad grin. Nobody told me to go to bed, so I hung around awhile.

After she'd slipped out of her sandals and settled on the couch with him, she asked about the parole board. "You never told me what restrictions they put on you."

He took a quick glance at me. I concentrated on drinking my Pepsi. I knew he didn't like to talk about prison around me.

"Oh, just the usual things," he finally told her.

"What usual things?" she insisted.

"I can't associate with ex-felons, and . . ." He stopped to finish peeling the label off his bottle of beer. "And I'm not to be found with anything in my possession that I can't show a proof of purchase for. Not even a ballpoint pen, they said."

"Is Rattler out?" Mom asked.

"I don't know," Dad said.

"Well, you better stay away from him."

Rattler wasn't the problem, I thought to myself. I finished my pop and said good-night. On the way out of the room, I gave the sandals a sneaky kick. They landed under the lamp table where I couldn't see them anymore.

I lay in bed a long time before going to sleep. The sadness that hung on me kept my eyes wide open. I loved my dad, but something was wrong with him. Why did he keep stealing things? Especially when he knew he might go back to prison.

17

Wishing on the North Star

I checked my Swatch. It was almost time for the bus. "Walk faster, Grace," I told her. "We're late."

"I know," she said, half running beside me. "I was working on my mom this morning."

"You look like you've been crying."

"I was. I had to do something to make her give me a bike."

"You cried!" We'd reached the bus stop and I turned to gape at her.

"Well, what was I supposed to do? What if you go off on your bike every day and I'm left all alone?"

"I've been left alone plenty of times and I never cried about it."

"Your dad gave you a ten-speed."

"My dad isn't perfect," I said, and climbed on the bus.

Grace went to the back to join her friends. I sat down next to the little kid with the big glasses. "Do you know Edward Troller?" I asked him.

The kid gave me an owly-eyed stare. "Who doesn't?"

"Well, I haven't seen him around lately."

"He got kicked out of school," the kid said. "And I'm glad."

"What'd he get kicked out for?"

"Stealing, probably. Or beating up someone who wouldn't give him lunch money. Who cares? He's gone." The kid turned to look out the window, which I guess was more interesting than answering my questions.

For the rest of the ride I thought about Troller getting kicked out. What was going to happen to him? He was only in the fourth grade. He couldn't be put in reform school, could he?

When I got home from school, the car was gone and the house was empty. Since it was Mom's day off, I didn't need to worry about Dad getting in trouble. But then I wondered if she thought the same thing when he was with me.

I made myself a sandwich out of barbecued beef and sagged down on the couch to eat it. I was beat because I hadn't slept much the night before. I'd kept thinking and thinking about my dad.

Would he stay out of trouble? Or get sent back up? He didn't seem to have learned much in jail. Troller never seemed to learn much either. He still ripped kids off no matter how many times Mrs. Nettle suspended him. Or for that matter, no matter how many times his old man beat him.

There was a loud banging at the door, which almost made me drop my sandwich. I don't like bangings.

Instead of opening the door, I peeked out the front window. Grace's blue eyes peeked through the pane back at me. "Chicken!" she yelled. "Come on out and see what I got."

"I'm eating!" I yelled back.

"Eat out here. I have something to show you."

I opened the door and went outside. Grace had a red girl's bike leaning against our front steps. "Jeez, that was fast," I said.

"I know. Mom found it advertised in the want ads. We just came back from buying it."

I pulled the bike up with the hand that wasn't holding my sandwich. "Looks neat."

"Well, it's only a five-speed. And it's got those dumb straight handlebars."

"That's okay," I told her. "Now at least you have wheels. Can you ride it?"

"A little bit." Grace was eyeing my sandwich. "That looks good."

"It is." I tore off a hunk and handed it to her.

She took a bite. "What is it?"

"Barbecued beef. My mom brings stuff home from the restaurant in doggie bags."

Grace's eyes bugged at her piece of sandwich. "You mean people's leftovers?"

"No, stupid. The health department would shut them down. She brings home stuff people don't order and the cook can't use the next day."

"Oh." Grace finished the last bite, wiped her hands on her jeans, and stuck a helmet on her head. "Let's go for a ride."

We rode down Highway 2 to the park that runs

125

along the Pilchuck River. I kept having to slow down for Grace. She was wobblier than my dad.

When we got to the park, Grace jumped off her bike, yanked the helmet off, and wiped her forehead with her arm. "That helmet is too hot."

"How come you're wearing it, then?"

"My mom makes me."

It's my opinion that Grace's mother ruins her. That helmet looked dorkier than the ribbons. I decided not to tell her this, though. Instead, I parked my bike and walked down to the bank of the river.

Grace sat on one of the big rocks beside me. "The river isn't very high for January," she said.

I tossed some pebbles into the water. "No, and it's sure warm for January."

"My dad says the weather in the Northwest is changing. He says if we don't get more rain, the growers in Eastern Washington are going to lose all their apple trees because there won't be enough water to irrigate. Matt says this is the shortest skiing season he can ever remember."

I didn't bother answering her. I like it when it doesn't rain. The sky's blue, the grass is green, and everything shines in the sun.

"Look at Mount Rainier," Grace said. "It looks like a dish of vanilla ice cream."

I looked across the valley at the huge white mountain. "Ya, except there's no dish. Come on, let's go back."

Grace left her helmet hanging on one of the handlebars when she climbed on her bike. I started out behind her, but she was going too slow. I circled around

126

some trees until I got the idea to ride ahead and come back down the path facing her.

I did just that. I pumped fast, keeping my head below the tree branches, until I had a twenty-yard lead. Then, I turned onto the path and zoomed for her.

"Whoa!" she hollered.

I kept coming. She kept coming. Grace hung in there until I was about a yard and a half away. Then she swerved.

"Chicken!" I screamed at her, doing a donut in the dirt.

"Okay, okay, we're even," she said over her shoulder as I drew up behind her.

We were still laughing when we got to Highway 2. I didn't notice her mom's car, but Grace did. She slowed and reached for her helmet. It was too late. Her mom pulled to the side of the road, rolled down her window, and called across the highway, "Grace Elliott! You get on your helmet right now or I'm taking that bike away."

Grace hurriedly fastened the helmet on her head.

"And leave it on!" Mrs. Elliott jerked her mad face inside the window and started up her car. Grace and I eased up the road away from her.

"What's your mom doing down this way?" I yelled back to Grace.

"She's taking her cat to the vet's."

I slowed my pace so we could keep on talking. "I didn't know you had a cat. I've never seen one at your house."

"She hides in Mom's room when there's company.

127

The only person she likes is Mom. She scratches me and Matt if we try to pick her up. And she goes to Mom and meows if we whack her back."

"Some pet."

We turned off Highway 2 onto our street. There wasn't much traffic, so we rode side by side. When we reached my house, Grace slid down from her seat and bumped her bike up the curb. "How about going riding after school tomorrow?"

"Okay," I agreed.

"Or did you want to see Pete?"

"No," I told her, "I'll go there on Saturday."

I was ready to ride up to my porch steps. I expected Grace to move over to her yard. Instead she stood quietly straddling her bike. Her head was tilted down with the stupid helmet shading her face. "I'm not doing anything Saturday," she said in a little voice.

"Let's go together, then."

Grace lifted her head. Her blue eyes smiled. "I'll bring a couple cans of pop."

"Bring one for Pete too. And maybe some cookies?"

"Right," she said and took off for her house.

Mom and Dad got home about a half hour after I did. They were loaded down with groceries. "You're going to make another whole dinner?" I asked Mom.

"Don't be smart," she said and whisked into the kitchen with her packages.

Dad dumped his bags on the dining room table and went out for more. I heaved off the couch and helped him stash the vegetables and milk in the refrigerator. When we were done, he asked me, "How about keeping me company on the porch?"

I got my jacket and went out and sat next to him on the top step. He was lighting up a cigarette. Mom says they give her headaches, so mostly he comes outside to smoke.

"Warm today, huh?" I said.

Dad nodded. "Ya, it seemed like the birds should be singing. When I was . . . um . . . on the inside, I used to look out my window the first spring. Flocks of crows would come by. They'd be screeching their heads off. Then swallows would whirl by. They all looked so free out there.

"Then when the birds came the next year, I could hardly stand it. I knew you were growing taller and older and I was missing every change. And I worried that maybe when I got out, I'd be a stranger to you."

Dad drew in on his cigarette, making it glow in the dark. He reached out his hand and knocked the ash into the garden dirt beside the steps. Then he seemed to shake himself into a cheerful mood. "Those are good-looking sandals you got Lily."

"Ya, I guess," I mumbled. The sandals were the last thing I wanted to talk about.

"She said you got them on a sale. My twenty was enough, huh?"

"I didn't use your twenty for that. I used it for the candy and for a barrette I gave the girl next door." Now you've done it, I told myself. You shouldn't have said that.

He started out teasing. "Oh, the girl next door

. . ." Then he suddenly stopped. "How'd you . . . how'd you get the sandals?"

I knew I'd blown it. I could try to joke about the discount like I'd done with Grace. But it didn't seem funny anymore.

"What did you use for money?" he insisted.

I couldn't think of anything fast so I sort of laughed and spread my fingers in front of his face. "Got them with my five-finger discount."

He sprang back from my hand. "You . . . Oh, no!"

"It wasn't a big deal," I assured him quickly. "They couldn't catch me."

When he was able to answer, his voice sounded like it was coming from the dead. "Prisons are full of guys they couldn't catch." He leaned over his knees, and for a minute I thought he was going to puke. Then he straightened and looked up at the sky as if he was searching for the stars behind the drifting clouds.

"Listen, son," he said in the same dead voice. "Listen real careful. Ugly, evil things happen in prison. They're mean places. Things happen in there that you're better off never knowing about. I'd rather kill myself than have you do time in the joint."

A shiver ran through me. I didn't know what the ugly things were, but he was scaring me anyway.

"Please. Please. You don't want to turn out like your old man."

"Okay," I said quickly. "I . . . I just wanted her legs to get better."

"I know." Dad took a long drag on his cigarette. It was my turn to pull back. His face in the light of the burning ash looked dented and sad. Like a Halloween pumpkin that had caved in with age.

In my mind I saw Reverend Elliott's firm mustached face. And Grace's plump face. . . .

Dad put his arm around my shoulders and I could feel his love for me. "Listen," he said. "Listen. Let's wish on the North Star. Let's wish that we'll both always be straight. All right?"

"All right," I said. "But I don't know where it is. The Big Dipper twisted around in the sky since I last looked."

We got off the porch steps and stood out in the grass, craning our heads at the stars. "There it is," Dad said, pointing at a bright speck between the clouds. "Let's wish."

We stood silently together making our wishes. I wasn't sure in my heart if he could keep his. But I knew I would keep mine.